MW01591748

Crazytown:

The Witch Tree

Jon Grilz

DEDICATION

To my mom, of course.

ACKNOWLEDGMENTS

Cover Art by:
Christian Masnaghetti
www.chrismasna.deviantart.com

Edited by:
Autumn Conley
autiej@gmail.com

Fer readin' with a red pen:
Faith Hansen

For bringin' the whiskey…and readin':
Michelle Struss

Prologue

Waves crashed against the rocks just feet from where he walked, but Scott couldn't see them in the ink black night. If not for the sound and the gentle spray from the ice cold water, there would be no way to know exactly how far from the edge he was. The moon was hidden away behind the clouds and the sky was threatening rain. In a word, the weather was horrible. It had been an unusually warm Minnesota autumn and the clicking sound of swirling dead leaves against rock made everything feel all the more surreal.

Just ahead of him was Tanya. Beautiful Tanya. Beautiful Tanya dressed all in black from head to toe. The red highlights in her dyed black hair were invisible under the stormy sky, but Scott had noticed them immediately when he'd picked her up in his dad's pickup truck.

He had sat there in the idling vehicle, watching through the rearview mirror, waiting to see her creep around the corner of her parents' house toward her waiting ride. His heart was pounding at the thought of being caught, but it beat even faster when he caught glimpse of her gliding across the lawn. She was grounded for breaking curfew and not allowed to be out of the house after school, yet there she was, doing as she pleased. *God, she's so cool*, he thought.

He first noticed the red highlights when she hopped up and slid into the bench seat next to him. He didn't dare compliment her, knowing it would only result in her rolling eyes and telling him to shut up, but Scott always noticed things about her: her icy blue eyes lined with black, the piercings in her nose and eyebrow, and the fact that she was always so dark and aloof... and beautiful.

As they made their way to the predetermined meeting place, she walked several steps ahead of him on the uneven ground. Her silhouette was only visible because of the beam from the Mag-lite she aimed ahead of them to illuminate their path.

"Keep up, Drake!" she snapped at him as he stumbled and grunted along.

He knew he should have been watching where he was going, especially on such a tumultuous trek, but instead his eyes were helplessly glued to her.

"Sorry," he said. Scott did his best to make his voice sound sure, but it always seemed to crack at the worst times, especially when Tanya called him 'Drake'. He was supposed to call her 'Shadow', but when she wasn't around, he always thought of her as who she really was, Tanya.

For several more minutes, the couple tripped and stumbled along, working their way through the labyrinth of trees and along the water's edge that opened up into the freezing, churning Lake Superior.

"Come on! Keep up! We're almost there," Tanya hissed back at him.

Scott knew she was only acting tough. She was as new to all of it as he was. If he wanted, he could probably still return his clothes to the Hot Topic at the Miller Hill Mall in Duluth. *I know I've still got the receipts somewhere,* he pondered with each frustrating step. He didn't normally dress that dark, gothic way, but Tanya had been adamant that it was important for the ritual. He wondered how much she really knew or if she was just repeating what she'd heard from Vlad.

Finally, the flashlight beam stopped bouncing and Scott heard Tanya let out a breathy whisper. "We're here."

The light slowly panned upward, eventually illuminating the demonic-looking claw that was the Witch Tree. Its roots twisted and wrapped around the rocks, as if it was growing straight out of them. The crooked formation didn't look natural, as if it had been warped by the Hand of God Himself.

"You can turn off that light. You won't need it."

Scotty jumped and turned while Tanya let out a little *eek*. Vlad had appeared from out of nowhere. He wore a long, black hooded cloak with a red pentagram embroidered on the back. The hood was low on his brow, almost completely covering his eyes and Scotty couldn't see Vlad's face, but he knew it was him.

When the flashlight had momentarily captured him, Tanya said hi to him in a voice far more lilting that she ever used when speaking to Scott. Then she turned off the light and the three were once again covered in the thick darkness. Tanya was always talking about how cool Vlad was, completely in awe of all the stuff he knew about the occult and Black Masses. She had met him online about a month earlier and split her online time between chatting with Scott and Vlad, even though Scott had been corresponding online with her for almost a year.

Scott had never personally met Vlad, but Tanya trusted him and Scott trusted Tanya. Now that he'd seen him in person, he realized Vlad wasn't anything special. The way Tanya talked about him, he was some kind of giant, but in reality, he was about the same height and build as Scott. In the end, Scott just kept reminding himself that it was all just an act anyway.

There was going to be other people there, it was all just for fun. He was aware that some people took things too seriously, but he was willing to play along—for Tanya.

The first flicker of light that Scott saw after Tanya turned off her flashlight was the spark from Vlad's lighter. Immediately after, a sudden *crack* of lightning set aglow the area with a haunting, eerie white-blue light. Vlad moved around the Witch Tree lighting large candles.

"Hey," Scott said. "I thought there were supposed to be more people here."

Vlad continued to focus his attention on lighting the candles and didn't bother to look at Scott as he spoke. "There will be, Drake. We can't do the ceremony without them." His voice was flat and harsh, as if he'd been smoking for longer than his own lifetime.

Tanya watched Vlad intently, taking notice of his every move and hanging on his every word. Scott watched Tanya with the same kind of interest, and when she shivered from a gust of wind, he put his arm around her to warm her up.

"Drake, knock it off," she said, pushing his arm away with an irritated huff.

Scott was quickly tiring of the whole scenario and thinking again about where he'd put those Hot Topic receipts, but then he saw two more people walking up from the trail through the woods. The boy and girl seemed to be the same age as Scott and Tanya. Tanya nodded in their direction as if she knew them, though Scott had no idea who they were. They nodded back.

By the time Vlad managed to light all the candles and keep them burning at the same time, there were a total of eight people standing around him—all pairs consisting of one boy, one girl. They all appeared to be high school age, and everyone was dressed in black from head to toe.

Vlad kept his head down as he stood up and slowly extended his arms out to the side. More lightning crackled through the sky, as if on cue.

"We are here today, because we are meant to be here." Vlad's voice boomed across the sky, even over the roar of waves that had begun to slam against the rock with growing violence.

"We are here because of the darkness that light-dwellers refuse to accept."

Spread out in a semi-circle around Vlad and the Witch Tree, the others began to sway like cobras hypnotized by a snake charmer.

"We are here, on this spot, because dark forces conspire and we will do their bidding."

The sky roared again, and Scott felt the first few drops of rain break through the clouds.

"Will you give yourselves over to the darkness? Will you accept that darkness into your own black hearts?"

After asking for such oaths, Vlad extended his hand out and turned in a circle, pointing at each person around him. All the while, more rain hit the ground, one by one putting out the candle flames.

The other people were rocking in the midst of some kind of rapture and responding, "Yes, yes, yes, yes," over and over again in a most unnerving chant.

"Then let us begin again what was started long ago..." Vlad's voice trailed off and the rain began to fall harder. All the candles were snuffed out with hissing fizzles as Vlad pulled back his hood.

A massive streak of lightning split the sky, turning night into day for the briefest of moments. In that moment, Scott saw Vlad's hoodless face and it was only in that moment that Scott, aka Drake, realized he'd made the gravest of mistakes.

CHAPTER 1

Darren Lockhart didn't make a move. His eyes were steel. His hands hung loose, but were ready for any immediate and sudden motion—or so he thought.

Before he knew how it had happened, an arm was around his throat. Lockhart grabbed at the large forearm and bicep, trying to create space to breath, but the grip was like a boa constrictor. There was no room to move, no room to inhale. His air and blood were being cut off and there was nothing he could do about it.

As the walls started to close in around his eyes, just as he was starting to lose consciousness, he let go of the arm and slapped the ground hard, twice.

The grip loosened and Lockhart fell free to the ground.

He rolled onto his back with a cough. "Damn! Every time."

His eyes were blurry for a moment, but when they finally cleared he saw a hand extended down, offering to help him to his feet. He grabbed it and lifted himself up with a huff. Lockhart groaned and cracked his neck to the side. "You know what? I think I might be getting too old for this game."

Lockhart's Brazilian jiu-jitsu instructor laughed and gave him a slap on the shoulder.

Since being transferred from the FBI to the position of chief of the Crayton Minnesota Police, under less than clear circumstances, Lockhart had taken it upon himself to do all he could to stave off boredom. In just under five weeks, he'd found that the joys of small-town living were best enjoyed in small doses.

Crayton was populated by less than 700 people, and other than himself and a deputy, the Crayton police consisted of only two volunteers. His duties tended to be limited to minor domestic disputes, the occasional drunken argument and serving as the honorary Grand Marshal of local sporting events.

So, to occupy his body and mind with something a bit more inspiring than drunken locals, domestic disturbances and high school basketball heroes, three times a week, for about an hour, Lockhart would make the thirty minute drive to Bemidji to practice Brazilian jiu-jitsu. It was a good way to stay in shape that didn't involve the same hard pounding on his knees as running, not to mention he'd always been a fan of mixed martial arts. *How hard can it be?,* he figured when he decided to sign up. He'd learn soon enough that the answer to that question was, *pretty dang hard.*

With a teacher who was a former MMA champ and black belt, he learned pretty fast that there was nothing easy about it. Nevertheless, he did enjoy it, and besides the exercise and excuse to get out a bit, jiu-jitsu also afforded Lockhart a greater knowledge of choke-holds and joint locks, something he found infinitely useful during long Sundays filled with pro football rivalries or sometimes even the occasional high school football rivalry.

Lockhart walked over to the side of the grappling mat, his traditional gi uniform soaked with sweat, and grabbed his water bottle. He looked forward to the day when he wouldn't be such an easy target, but at over forty, he wasn't sure that day would ever come.

Before he was able to step back onto the mat,

Lockhart turned back at the sound of his phone vibrating inside of his gym bag.

"Lockhart," he answered as he wiped sweat from his forehead.

"Hey Chief," said his deputy and local chef, Freddie Lind.

"Hey Freddie. What's up? I thought you were working at the café today?" As he said the words, Lockhart knew something was wrong.

"Yeah, I am," Lind answered, "but I just heard that Scott Erickson hasn't been seen since last night. His parents called into the office but Dean didn't know what to do."

Lockhart chewed on his lower lip. It was a tough situation and he wasn't really surprised to hear that the other volunteer deputy was clueless as to how to handle it. Technically, no one was to be considered officially missing until they'd been gone at least twenty-four hours, but big-city protocol and procedures manuals held little weight in small-town communities where everyone seemed to know everyone else's whereabouts most of the time.

"I'll be there in half an hour."

Lockhart bowed out to the instructor and excused himself. He took just a moment to shower before putting on his police blues. The uniform itself had actually been one of the more difficult adjustments to make after his transfer from the FBI to police the small Northern Minnesota town. Lockhart preferred the typical FBI garb, suits, ties and tailored shirts. The general-issue blue uniform and black pants left little room for any kind of fashion statement.

Lockhart's drive quickly took him from the more populated streets of Bemidji to the quiet expanse of forest he now called home. The drive always seemed to blink by. Waves of green flowed past his police cruiser windows as his mind drifted to the Erickson family.

He hadn't been in Crayton long enough to put faces to names automatically and there was more than one Erickson family in town. Instead of guessing, Lockhart called into the law enforcement office to talk with the receptionist, Joy.

"Crayton Law Enforcement. This is Joy. How can I help you?" Joy's matronly tone was always sweet and cheerful, quite true to her name.

"Hi Joy. It's Darren," Lockhart had been on a first name basis with Joy since he first met her a month prior and had taken up residence in her bed-and-breakfast while investigating the Mikey Weber murder, back when he was still a FBI agent and still allowed to wear his much-loved suits to work.

"Oh, hi Chief! How was the gym?"

"Fine, thanks. I got a call from Deputy Lind. He said the Erickson family hasn't seen their son since last night, and—"

"Yeah, we got the call about an hour ago," she cut in. "—Dean was here, but he's never dealt with a missing person before."

"It's okay Joy. Is Dean around?"

"Nope. He's out watching the football practice."

Lockhart shook his head, still amazed at the small town's mass addiction to high school sports. Technically, Dean wasn't doing anything wrong; he was a volunteer after all, and he could virtually come and go as he pleased. Nevertheless, the chief had some questions for Dean—and for Joy in the meantime.

"Hey Joy, what are Scott's parents' names?" Lockhart asked.

"Jess and Justin. They live about a block down from Freddie."

"Got it. Thanks Joy."

Joy's voice grew serious, concerned, "Do you think anything happened to Scott?"

"No Joy. I'm sure the boy's just taken a short field trip for his own reasons and will be back before dinner. Still, it's good to follow up on these things. It comes with the job." Lockhart hung up his phone and felt bad about lying to Joy.

CHAPTER 2

FBI Agent Caitlyn Rhodes wasn't a fan of heights, and even with 100 feet of rock between her and the cliffs edge she felt uneasy. It was only twenty or so feet over the water, but it might as well have been a mile.

Regardless of her knee-length, black wool coat and leather gloves, she felt the bitter Lake Superior wind blow through her as she investigated the scene. She opted to leave it to the forensics team to do their end of the investigation, by the cliff, while she interviewed David Crowe.

"One more time please, Mr. Crowe," Caitlyn said through her barely open mouth.

"My story ain't gonna change, no matter how much you Feds want it to. I'm full-blooded Ojibwe and I have rights like anybody else." David Crowe stood at least eight inches taller than Caitlyn, dressed in a blue flannel shirt and faded blue jeans, and he didn't seem nearly as affected by the cold. He had a strong, square jaw and unblinking, almost-black eyes. His long black hair was tied back in a single braid that ran half-way down his back.

"I haven't accused you of anything, Mr. Crowe. I just need the facts," Caitlyn said, holding her ground.

Crowe flexed his jaw. "Like I said, at ten this morning I guided a group of tourists here to see the Witch Tree." Crowe motioned over to the small, twelve-foot tree. Despite the infamously vicious Minnesota winters and freezing lake winds, the oddly-shaped three, like something out of a horror film, was estimated to have lived over 300 years. "Because stupid tourists kept vandalizing our sacred land, this place is off limits to anyone without an Ojibwe guide. We have to prevent careless fools from desecrating our land any further."

Caitlyn could see Crowe's anger snowballing the more he spoke and she did her best to shift the mood of the conversation. "Yes sir, I understand. Please tell me what happened once you arrived."

Crowe eyed Rhodes and sighed heavily. His massive chest swelled with the breath. "It looked just like you see it. Some idiot soiled our land with candles in some kind of devil ceremony."

"How do you know it had anything to do with, as you put it, the 'devil'?" Caitlyn asked in an attempt to back Crowe into a corner.

Crowe was as bright as he was tall and didn't bite. "It isn't the first time. Stupid white kids with too much time come here and have their ceremonies thinking they are vampires or werewolves or something stupid."

"Our records don't indicate any reports of similar incidents in the past, Mr. Crowe. What made you call in the report this time?" Caitlyn obviously already knew the answer, but she needed her witness—and possible suspect— to say it out loud for the record.

Crowe shifted and rolled his shoulders. He looked uncomfortable. "Because of the *blood*."

Agent Rhodes had inched her way out to see it for herself when she'd first arrived on the scene. There was, in fact, a blood-stain near the lip of the ledge, but patrol boats had been unable to find anything in the way of a body or any additional blood on the rocks below. Her first instinct had been that someone had slipped, hit their head and rolled into the churning water.

Caitlyn kept her focus on David Crowe, who had started to look more and more uncomfortable.

"Is there something wrong Mr. Crowe? You seem...
nervous," she said, realizing her tone was more smug
than she intended.

Crowe shifted his jaw back and forth. "I *am*
nervous. You find blood here today and tomorrow you
find out it belonged to some privileged white kid. The
day after that there'll be dozens of agents picking over
this land and taking it from us—again."

Caitlyn remained unfazed. "What makes you think
we'll discover, as you put it, that the blood came from
'some privileged white kid'?"

Crowe leaned a little closer to Caitlyn, till his body
was looming immensely over hers, completely dwarfing
her. "Because only white kids are dumb enough to
trespass here."

Agent Rhodes held her ground without so much as
a single muscle twitch. "And the privileged part? How
do you know the blood came from someone
privileged?"

Crowe sneered and leaned back. "Because, Agent,
they're white."

Rhodes knew, there was no point in continuing her
line of questioning with Crowe. His story hadn't
changed, and he was growing angrier with every new
inquiry. For Caitlyn's part, she thought maybe he had
every right to be. He wasn't wrong about what could
happen to the land; the investigation of a possible
death would inevitably outweigh the Bureau's concern
for the land itself. In turn, that would be met with
protest that could reach across the nation.

Agent Rhodes took Crowe's information and told
him not to leave town. The big man shook his head
dismissively and walked back into the woods in the
direction of his parked truck. Once he was gone, Caitlyn

turned her attention to the scene investigators for an update.

The preliminary investigation resulted in the discovery of six different sets of footprints. By the length and widths of those prints, they estimated three men and three women. There had been a hard rain the night before, making it difficult to distinguish the exact path the six trespassers had taken to and from the scene. Even more so, it also suggested that there had been significant blood loss in that there was still red-stained rock despite the precipitation.

The candles that encircled the tree were hardly melted, and not much wax had dried on the rocks, so Caitlyn figured it safe to assume the rain had started not long into whatever was going on, but hadn't gotten hard until the blood had some time to dry. Reports from the National Weather Service indicated that the rain had probably begun at midnight, which aligned well with Crowe's occult ritual theory. Along with that, statistically, both the act and local population suggested that white kids were the major players.

The wind picked up again and Caitlyn hugged her coat tightly around her body. Her ears and nose filled with hot needles from the bitter cold kiss. Her eyes watered slightly as she looked out to the restless waters. Hundreds of sailors had lost their lives over the years and a kid might have just been added to the list. She had six people to find, ideally all alive.

Agent Caitlyn Rhodes pulled out her cell phone, shielded the mouthpiece from the wind and called in to the FBI field office for a list of recent missing persons reports.

CHAPTER 3

It was the second time in two days that Crayton Chief of Police Darren Lockhart had been to the Erickson household. The day before, it had been a routine visit, just swinging by on his way home from the gym to check in about their son not being seen in a while. The second visit was anything but routine.

Jess and Justin Erickson sat on the couch opposite Lockhart, holding hands. They were a young couple, in their mid-to-late thirties, but they had a seventeen-year-old son.

Above and behind where the Ericksons sat was a family portrait of the three of them. Lockhart could see that Scott was the spitting image of his father. They both had the same sandy brown hair and toothy, squinting smiles. They shared narrow shoulders and rosy red cheeks. Jess was a short woman, maybe five-two, with her blonde hair pulled back into a loose braid and a look of longing in her eyes.

Lockhart had met the two in passing a couple of weeks prior, but they could hardly be recognized as the same people. Their faces were drained and showed almost no color. Both sets of eyes were sad and as he spoke with them, they stared into the distance in quiet reservation.

The day before, Lockhart had asked the basic questions about where Scott might be. They had no idea. Scott had taken the truck out to go meet some friends after dinner. As his room was in the basement, it wasn't abnormal for him to come home without their hearing him come in. In the morning, they had woken up to find both Scott and Justin's nineties-model Chevy pickup still gone.

There had been no sign of Scott or the truck for two days and it was clear that the parents were terrified, which Lockhart couldn't fault them for. They were doing their best to convince themselves that he'd just run off—that it was all some act of teenage rebellion. As much as Lockhart wished he could set their hearts at ease by agreeing with them; he wasn't so sure that was the case.

His first instinct was more than rebellion. Crayton had its share of rebellious youths, but Scott wasn't one of them. His parents had mentioned that the boy had started wearing all black as of late and listening to "that music," but the rebellion theory still didn't sit right with Lockhart. One thing was for sure: no drugs had been found. A search of his computer, with the parents' permission, didn't turn anything up, but there was always the possibility that Scott had cleared his history and cookies to keep his parents—or anyone else—from seeing his favorite cyberspace haunts.

Jess looked too lost to speak and in her eyes hung a shimmering layer of restrained tears.

Seeing his wife on the brink, Justin spoke for them both. "Have you heard anything new, Chief?"

Lockhart refrained from shifting in his seat, but he felt nervous. The transition to local police hadn't been an easy one. Among other things, it meant that he had to get to know people on a personal level. He had to know their lives and be that constant light they could turn to in their moments of darkness.

"We haven't heard anything, but Scott's description is out on the wire and we've contacted the state police about your truck."

The Ericksons looked at each other for a moment and shared a tense silence before Justin spoke again.

"Uh, Chief, we were just wondering, because…well, you know, you used to be with the FBI…" he stuttered.

And there it was. Lockhart knew it wouldn't go away easily, but he also hadn't expected it to come up so quickly. To them he was still an agent who could make a phone call and get the federal government involved. He moved forward to the edge of his chair and looked around at all the family pictures.

"Please believe me, we… I am doing everything possible to get Scott home. It's just that sometimes, these things take a while. I want to be honest with you. Because there are no signs of violence and your truck is still missing, we are still working under the assumption that Scott left on his own accord."

Jess finally felt compelled to speak up. "Scott wouldn't do this! He wouldn't scare us like this. Something's wrong." She broke down crying and buried her face in her husband's chest, and Justin gently and tenderly patted her head to console her.

Lockhart's phone vibrated and he discreetly glanced down at the caller ID. It was a number he hadn't seen since he had first showed up in Crayton: the Duluth FBI office. Lockhart felt a lump in his throat as he excused himself and stepped onto the Ericksons front porch.

"Lockhart."

"Chief Lockhart? This is Agent Caitlyn Rhodes with the FBI. I tried calling you at the police station, but your receptionist said you were out and gave me your personal cell number." Her voice was smoky and had a comical tone in regards to Joy's openness to sharing his private number.

Lockhart sighed. "Yeah, Joy does that. What can I do for you, Agent?"

"You filled out a missing person's report on a Scott Erickson yesterday. Is that correct?"

Lockhart's heart sank. "Yes."

"In that case, I believe we need to talk—the sooner the better."

CHAPTER 4

FBI Agent Caitlyn Rhodes had spent ten of her twelve years with the Bureau in Minnesota, and in all that time she couldn't remember ever having been to Crayton. Having been assigned to Duluth for most of that time made it all the more strange. She had been to, or through, Northhome, Blackduck, Bemidji and several other area cities, but it seemed like Crayton had always stayed off her radar.

Evidently it stayed off her GPS, too, because she drove right around the town without even realizing it, and the electronic voice on her navigator said nary-a-word. She finally found the single-lane road that led through the woods into the small town of Crayton, population 639, according to the sign.

There wasn't anything to it. Crayton looked like any other of a number of northern Minnesota towns: small population, high bar-to-patron ratio. The city was built largely around a series of three crossroads. If anything, it seemed to be its own little world, surrounded and cradled by forests of green, gold and red. The changing seasons made that particular part of the country beautiful in ways that Caitlyn's words could not even begin to adequately describe.

Caitlyn loved autumn: the cool air, Sunday touch football games with friends and Honey Crisp apples, her personal favorite of all that Minnesota had to offer.

Agent Rhodes's Town Car rolled slowly through the Crayton streets as she kept an eye out for the police station. What she found was a two-story house with a "Law Enforcement Office" sign in the front yard.

On the front porch swing sat an officer, in a black and blue uniform with his eyes focused down at a file folder that lay open in his lap. Though she'd never met the man in person, she assumed he was Darren Lockhart. His reputation had preceded him and she'd wondered more than once what he had done to get transferred to a local police force after being a FBI special agent in charge of violent crimes.

Rhodes parked her car in front of the office and stepped into the vacant street. "This place isn't easy to find. I drove right past it," she announced.

Lockhart looked up casually and stood to greet her with an outstretched hand. "Yeah, it happens. Agent Rhodes, I presume?"

She nodded. "Chief Lockhart?"

He nodded.

Lockhart was taller than she thought he would be. Normally, at five-ten, she was able to look other agents in the eyes, if not down at them—especially wearing heels, but Lockhart still stood two inches taller than her. She knew from his file that he was forty-two, but he didn't look it. He was fit, though his demeanor suggested he was already starting to slow from his days in the field. He had broad shoulders and didn't slouch. His soft blue eyes never broke contact with hers.

Even in the twenty-first century, the FBI still felt like a boys club and Caitlyn had gotten used to men looking her up and down to size her up. She avoided much of it by dressing conservatively. Her hair was up or pulled back to a pony tail. She almost exclusively wore pantsuits and never flaunted or used her sexuality. She knew what kind of jokes were told at her expense, but she didn't care. She had a job to do, and she did it well, in spite of being 'the fairer sex' and in spite of all the whispers and giggles she heard when she walked past a herd of her male colleagues.

There was something different about Lockhart's look, and it took a moment for Caitlyn to realize that he was just waiting for her to speak.

She went on, "Chief Lockhart, I'm currently working on an investigation that I think may have a link to your missing teenager."

Without moving his eyes, Lockhart said, "Yeah, I know."

"But how..." Caitlyn stopped herself and looked down at the file folder in Lockhart's hand. "How did you get that?"

Lockhart's face seemed serene. "Agent, I hope you aren't offended by my curtness, but we both know who I am, I'm sure you're keenly aware of my newly found infamy in the department. Let's get past that. I'm not so far removed that I can't still get a case file. So please, let's not focus on who I am and what I've done, but instead on what's important. I've got two heartbroken young parents on my hands, and we have to find Scott Erickson."

Agent Rhodes appreciated his forwardness and could see there'd be no games with him. "Of course," she responded.

Lockhart stepped to the side of the front door. "Would you like to step inside and go over it?"

Caitlyn walked past him as he held the screen door open for her. "Do you live here?" she asked looking around the converted residence.

"No, but the deputy does," Lockhart said matter-of-factly.

"The deputy?"

"Yeah. Moved in after his house blew up. I live in the bed-and-breakfast up the hill."

Caitlyn quickly realized that the man was quite

funny in a strange way. He spoke so plainly that he was a difficult man to get a read on. Even as he took his seat behind his desk, there was a look of odd discomfort on his face. *Maybe transitioning to police work is more difficult than I thought.* Rhodes surmised.

Before Caitlyn got a chance to say anything, an older woman came in the front door with a plate covered in tinfoil. She had a warm smile on her face and said hello immediately.

"Hi," Caitlyn said. "You must be Joy. I'm Agent Rhodes. We spoke on the phone earlier."

"Oh hi! It's nice to meet you." Joy set the plate on Lockhart's desk and shook Caitlyn's hand firmly and enthusiastically. Then she turned to Lockhart. "Darren, we missed you at lunch. Jill put together a plate for you—some of last night's pot roast. Extra carrots, of course." Joy winked at him and Lockhart gave a blushing smile.

The police chief gets a wink for extra carrots? God, this is a weird little postage stamp.

Joy excused herself to other parts of the office and Lockhart motioned for Caitlyn to sit.

"Hungry?" he asked.

Caitlyn looked at the plate. "No, thank you."

Lockhart shrugged. "You don't know what you're missing. Jill is Joy's sister, and she's also the second best cook in town."

Caitlyn resisted asking who the best cook was. "I'm fine thanks."

Lockhart turned his attention to the plate. A plume of steam rose as he removed the foil. The smell of home cooking filled the office and Caitlyn was tempted to reconsider the offer. Lockhart made himself a sandwich out of roast meat, potatoes and a thick layer of carrots between two slices of white bread.

"Chief Lockhart, can we get back to the case?"

Lockhart's eyes, which had been focused on his sandwich lifted with new-found determination. "Agent, please don't mistake my casual behavior with a lack of urgency."

Caitlyn felt challenged by his sudden shift in mood, and she, herself, was never one to back down. "Hmm. Then in that case, Chief Lockhart, just what should I mistake it for?"

Lockhart took a bite of his sandwich and took his time chewing it thoroughly before he answered. He wiped his mouth with a bit of paper towel and said, "Apprehension."

Rhodes felt condescension coming. Male agents and cops always seemed to think they had a better take on the situation, as if women couldn't grasp investigations.

"Your report," Lockhart said, "has holes."

Caitlyn scoffed. "Oh? Is that right?"

Lockhart nodded as he leaned forward. "Yeah, that's right." He flipped open the file folder and spun it on the desk towards Agent Rhodes. "Your report indicates that some kind of party or ritual may have happened on the cliff edge. Wax pools were found, showing that candles were lit. Time was established based on weather patterns." Lockhart looked up. "Which, by the way, I was impressed with."

Caitlyn let a smirk slip out at the compliment, but she composed herself immediately.

Lockhart went on. "It was done around midnight, which I'm a little confused about, but I'll get back to that. The presence of six people was established. A bloodstain on the ledge, tested as type-A—a match for

Scott Erickson, by the way—suggests an accident or possible assault. The body was presumed lost in Lake Superior."

Caitlyn Rhodes leaned back in her chair. She was confused, if not apprehensive, about what Lockhart was going to say next. "Okay. Thanks for the recap, but just where do you think I went wrong?"

Lockhart's eyebrows twitched for a moment. He looked confused and didn't answer right away. "Not *wrong*, per se. It just feels too specific, like you are looking for an answer on a deadline. You report in terms of absolutes, and that takes away objectivity. Believe me, these things aren't always what they seem."

"Actually, Chief Lockhart, that is usually the case."

Lockhart shrugged dismissively. "Regardless, don't rule out something bigger."

"Something historic, perhaps?" Rhodes baited. She knew his old theory on the existence of the supposed Jack the Shooter and wanted to gauge his reaction on such a suggestion.

Lockhart simply went on as if he didn't seem to notice the jab.

"Scott's parents said he left after dinner two days ago. According to Google Maps, it would be a six-hour drive. How did you establish that *Scott* was actually there that night?"

"The drive wouldn't have been that bad on back roads. It might not have been the best route, but never underestimate a teenager's resolve. They can be...stubborn to the point of foolishness," Caitlyn said, thinking back on her own days of being young and too self-assured.

"I'll give you that much, but you are still forgetting

about the truck."

Caitlyn looked down at the file folder. "What truck?"

"Scott took his dad's truck. Was a vehicle found around the site?"

Caitlyn let out a hesitant, "No."

"Well, if we are going to assume this was an accident, where did his truck go? If the boy fell, that means someone had to take his truck to cover the tracks. That changes things. Also, if they were of the mindset to take the truck, why leave the blood stain? Doesn't make sense, if you ask me."

Agent Rhodes wanted to dismiss hare-brained theories, but she knew Lockhart was right; there were too many holes. She looked over at Lockhart, whose expression was still neutral. He took no pleasure in pointing out what she had overlooked; either that, or he was just good at hiding it.

"Okay, *Chief* Lockhart," she said almost condescendingly, "then what do you suggest?"

Lockhart looked at his watch then leaned to the side. "Hey Joy!" He called out. Joy's head popped around the corner. "Yeah, Chief?"

"Joy, Dean's on tonight too, right?"

"He sure is," she said with a smile. "Big game tonight, ya know."

Lockhart let out a chortle. "Of course. Thanks Joy. Let Dean know I need to take a personal day, but I'll have my cell on me if he needs anything."

Joy had a surprised look on her face and glanced between Lockhart and Caitlyn. "Oh, okay Chief. Will you be home for dinner tonight?"

Lockhart shook his head. "Probably not."

CHAPTER 5

The North Woods of Minnesota is a beautiful place to be any time of the year, but autumn makes everything particularly breath-taking. The trees reflect the passage of time. Their leaves like the setting sun, change to yellows and reds before the coming winter storms that will blanket everything in a heavy, unforgiving, layer of white, erasing life only to create anew months later.

There is poetry in the place that the man called Vlad wasn't capable of expressing, but he still loved it so. If nothing else, it afforded him the silence he wanted and needed—a silence that was constantly broken by the banging of bone on metal.

"Let me out of here you freak!"

It was the same threat or insult every time. *There is no originality in any of it, but what can one expect when you put a teenage boy into a cage?*

He walked from the window and crouched down to the cage, where the young man lay, curled up, unable to even sit up.

"Please stop yelling," the man the boy had known as Vlad said. "It makes me...tense. And I'm sure neither of us wants that, now do we?"

He then walked around the cage to look the boy in the eyes. Even with his head turned away, he was clearly terrified. To the boy's credit, he tried to put on as strong a front as he could.

"Now, I don't quite know what I'm going to do with you yet, but if I get too tense, my face will start to wrinkle." He leaned closer, his face almost pressed against the cage. "And if that happens...I'll just have to take yours."

CHAPTER 6

Lockhart didn't look forward to the five hour drive from Crayton to Grand Portage, especially since there was almost nothing to actually link Scott to whatever had gone on up there. Nevertheless, it did afford him an opportunity to change out of his police uniform, and he had to be thankful for small blessings.

Lockhart asked Agent Rhodes to give him ten minutes to change before they left. He didn't actually have jurisdiction outside of Crayton unless he could somehow actually and undeniably place Scott at the scene. Since he was actively investigating the disappearance of one of his citizens, he could at least act as an advisor on the case, one with extensive experience—under Agent Caitlyn Rhodes's supervision, of course.

His first impression of her had been one of competence. She was certainly driven, considering that she was willing to make the trip from her office in Duluth to Grand Portage to Crayton, only to possibly go back to Grand Portage for an investigation that could have been written off as an accident. He wondered if her trip to Crayton had anything to do with him. While he would have liked to think that he still had that kind of draw with women, he avoiding spending too much time deluding himself. After all, Agent Rhodes was an attractive woman, no matter how hard she tried to hide it. She was tall and blonde with bright emerald-green eyes, and she had strong confidence about herself. He was sure she probably had to deal with more than a few unwanted advances in the department, and Lockhart refused to be one of them; he knew better. She was there for the investigation and possibly because she was curious about his transfer from FBI field work to being a small town cop. It was far from the legacy he would have liked to have left with the Bureau, but it was what it was.

Lockhart turned his attention to his closet as Agent Rhodes stayed downstairs and chatted with Joy about how lovely the weather had been.

He pulled out his sleek-cut, gray Ralph Lauren suit. As seemed to be the trend, it was a bit of a throwback to the ever popular 1960s business man look: single-breasted with medium-sized notched lapels and an upper button at navel level. It just felt right to go through the process of tying a Windsor knot again, to see the perfect crease in his pants. While some might have felt it too constrictive or formal or stuffy, he felt more comfortable in that suit than in his loose-fitting cop uniform or even in a t-shirt and jeans. It made him feel important again, as if there was more meaning to his life than enforcing school-night curfews or pulling over teens for playing their truck radios too loudly.

Lockhart even put on his backup ankle holsters for old time's sake. He took one last look in the mirror, straightened his Giorgio Armani solid black neck tie and went downstairs.

Joy let out an, "Oh my, don't you look nice?" and for a moment he thought he saw Agent Rhodes's face lighten up, a rare change from what he had started to think was a permanent scowl. He wondered if that scowl reflected his own expression to non-agents when he had been on FBI investigations.

"All set?" he asked Agent Rhodes.

"Uh-huh," she said. "I hope you like driving."

And she wasn't kidding. As the crow flew, it would have been about a three-hour trip at most, but taking the main roads, they had to drive south before going north. They actually had to go almost all the way back to Silver Bay before turning left and heading up the North Shore.

They didn't speak much at first, and any attempts at casual conversations were limited to either the investigation or work history. After five hours of driving, with two pits stops for gas and coffee, all Lockhart had really learned about Agent Rhodes was that she was a ten-year veteran of the FBI after spending five years on the Dallas Texas police force. And she seemed to be a bit defensive, but to Lockhart, it seemed the best female federal officers usually were.

During the drive, Lockhart took the opportunity to find more out about the site of the disappearance. The so-called Witch Tree was a sacred symbol of the Ojibwe people who knew it as Little Cedar Spirit Tree. The earliest recorded mention of the tree went all the way back to the 1730s, courtesy of French explorers. It was thought to be a fully grown tree even back then, making it at least 300 years old. Offerings of tobacco were often left at the tree in exchange for safe journey on Lake Superior; however, because of vandalism, the area had been closed off to tourists, and just as Crowe had indicated, the only legal way to access the tree was in the company of an official Ojibwe guide.

Agent Rhodes had arranged to have David Crowe, the Ojibwe guide that originally reported the scene, to meet them there. She also made a point to tell Lockhart not to refer to him or his tribe as Chippewa, as they were more commonly known in the southern part of the state. Chippewa was an Anglicization of the Ojibwe name and she didn't want to create any potentially and unnecessary harsh feelings. Lockhart wondered why there should be any harsh feelings to start with, but he soon found out that there had already been some bad blood on the case—and it wasn't the blood that stained the rock.

The weather in Grand Portage was far colder than in Crayton. They were only about seven miles from Canada and the wind blew with a winter chill. The sky was a shroud of gray and all the color was drained from the landscape. Many of the trees were already mere skeletons of themselves and the ground was scattered with their lost leaves. The land was cold and unforgiving.

David Crowe stood beside a new, red, Ford F150 pick-up truck as Agent Rhodes and Chief Lockhart approached the ceremonial land. He shook Lockhart's hand and eyed Rhodes suspiciously.

"Crayton?" Crowe asked in response to Lockhart's identification. He looked Lockhart up and down, eyeing his suit. "What are you doing here?"

Lockhart didn't mince his words. "Agent Rhodes and I think there might be a link between what happened here and a teen missing from my town."

"I see," Crowe said solemnly. "I'm sorry for your loss." His eyes looked sad, as if he thought the missing person might be dead.

"I appreciate it, but don't be sorry unless we can't find him. Can you please take us to the scene?" Lockhart asked.

Crowe nodded. "Of course. This way, Mr. Lockhart."

He politely stepped aside for Lockhart and Lockhart stepped aside for Rhodes who just looked at both men. Lockhart shrugged at the Minnesota-standoff (three people all waiting for the other person to go first). "Suit yourself," he said, and then he led the way down the path to the Witch Tree.

The iconic arbor stood in stark contrast to the blue-gray horizon. The body of the tree looked painfully twisted, without rhyme or reason, as if it had grown directly out of the rocks. Around the base were small tufts of tobacco. The hardened wax remnants of the candles still clung to the ground in spots. The branches were warped with some kind of arboreal rigor. Leaves were perched on the top like a bad toupee. Near lifeless, the Ojibwe Spirit Tree stood like a silent, arthritic sentry upon the water.

Lockhart walked around the site and wandered precariously close to the edge of the cliff. It was an isolated place, and he imagined it was probably the type that would draw in those who believed in spirits and magic.

He looked back from the edge and saw Agent Rhodes still standing near the tree line. She didn't look like she wanted to step any further.

"Can't swim?" he asked.

Rhodes didn't answer.

Lockhart looked over the ledge and back again. "You know, it isn't that far of a drop."

She ignored him and turned to David Crowe. "Have you thought of anything else since we last spoke?"

"You drive all this way to ask me that? Never heard of a phone?" Crowe snapped. His contempt for whatever had gone on at the previous interview laced his words like poison.

"Actually," Lockhart said as he stepped between the two, "*I* wanted to come here. It helps me investigate if I can see the place where it happened. Pictures may speak a thousand words, but they still never do the actual scene justice."

David Crowe gave a small nod of agreement.

"How many people were here that night?" Lockhart asked.

"Scene investigators confirmed six sets of prints," Caitlyn said over his shoulder.

"Actually," Lockhart said without looking back at her, "I was asking Mr. Crowe."

Crowe's brow furrowed. "What's that supposed to mean? Another white man accusing me of a crime?"

Lockhart moved a step closer, his eyes wide and innocent, almost naïve. "Is that what it sounds like? I'm sorry. I didn't mean for it to sound that way. Let me try again." Lockhart looked back at the forest and traced a trail up to the tree. "When you got here with the tourists, and you saw the wax and blood, how many people were here? And you know I'm not talking about the tourists."

Crowe squinted, trying to size up the man standing across from him; Lockhart could see a flash of recognition and appreciation for another man who saw beyond the obvious, and he knew in that moment, he had gained the man's respect.

"Nine," Crowe finally said.

Lockhart repressed a smile. He turned to face Rhodes, whose mouth was slightly agape, her eyes slits of confusion. While still looking at her, he directed another question Crowe's way. "Anything else?"

Crowe when on, "At least four were teenagers and probably knew they were doing something wrong, even if they weren't actually involved in what happened."

Lockhart kept his eyes on Rhodes. She stared back coldly enough to make him forget about the frigid winds.

"How do you know that?" she asked. Lockhart saw her right hand twitch. She was ready to go for her gun, but he shook his head just slightly, indicating that it wasn't the time or the place for that.

"I'm full-blooded Ojibwe and your backwaters lab doesn't know anything about tracking, in spite of all your fancy gadgets and gizmos. Two women walked in front, followed by two men in their footprints wherever there was mud or grass to be pressed down. If you would have bothered to look farther out, you woulda also see that only five people walked out—four women, one man.

Rhodes moved forward mechanically. Her eyes looked glazed over, and she wandered around the crime scene in an attempt to get a handle on the situation. The fact that in just a few minutes a small-town cop and a Native American guide had managed a complete upheaval of all the answers she thought the crime scene held was almost unnerving for her, not to mention humiliating.

Lockhart and Crowe stood in silence as she looked around, almost dumbfounded.

In the end, all Agent Rhodes was able to mutter was a meek and halfhearted, "What?"

CHAPTER 7

Agent Caitlyn Rhodes fumed as she drove her Town Car south, away from the Witch Tree, the "scene of the kidnapping" as Crayton Police Chief Darren Lockhart put it.

She was furious that he'd shown her up at the scene. She was angry that she'd driven five hours just to have her investigation turned on its head in ten minutes by a former FBI agent. And she was beyond pissed that Lockhart had refused to so much as gloat.

If he had done something as pathetic as apologize she would have lost all respect for him. If he had at least given her a little self-assured, victorious, I-told-you-so kind of smirk, though, she could have gotten mad and moved on. But Lockhart showed no emotion at all. All he did was sit there, his eyes focused out the side window as he listened to some music on his phone.

She couldn't be sure, but she thought it sounded like The Clash.

Caitlyn could only handle it all for about ten miles before she finally snapped. "What *are* you listening to?"

Lockhart turned his head with an expression like he wasn't sure she was talking to him, as if someone else were in the car. He removed an ear bud. "Sorry? What was that?"

"What are you listening to?"

"The Clash," he said matter-of-factly and put the ear bud back in.

Rhodes was dumbfounded. *Does he really think I only wanted to know what kind of music he's listening to? God, for some kind of talented investigator, he sure is slow.* "Hey!"

Lockhart removed his ear bud again. "Yeah?"

"Are we going to talk about it or what?"

"About what?" he asked.

"You railroaded me back there!" she said, seething.

Lockhart removed the other ear bud and coiled them around his phone. "I didn't railroad you."

"Oh yeah? Then what exactly was that little know-it-all show back there?"

He put his phone in his jacket pocket. "I was iust doing my job, Agent—investigating."

"Is that what you call it?"

Lockhart turned in his seat to look at her. His eyes were calm, but his look was serious. "Yes, I do. Now, I'm not sure what you have against me, or David Crowe, or the world for that matter, but you need to open your eyes a little wider and focus on finding the facts, even if that means swallowing your own pride a little."

Agent Rhodes jerked the steering wheel to the side, smacking Lockhart against the door. She slammed on the brakes and screeched to a stop on the side of the road. She threw the car into park and twisted her body to face him. "What the hell is your problem? You don't even know me, so what makes you think you can talk to me like that, *Chief*?"

Lockhart kept his cool. "Besides finding Scotty Erickson, I don't have a problem. Then again, I'm not that one who mistakenly assumed David Crowe guilty and thereby missed using him as an asset. I get it. Blame the Native, right? He had an attitude and was obviously touchy about people traipsing all over their sacred land. I probably would have had my suspicions too."

Caitlyn seethed. "Blame the Native? How dare you accuse *me* of being racist!"

Lockhart rolled his eyes. "Give me a break. This isn't about race. This is about you wanting to solve a crime as quickly as possible. You want an easy answer, and that answer just happened to be implicating Crowe. When you saw a chance of adding an assault and possible murder charge, you jumped at the opportunity. Then you find a missing persons report on a teen who lives in a town with a former agent with such a colorful and no doubt joke-worthy notoriety, and you just—"

"I..." Caitlyn stammered out, interrupting him.

"Save it. This has been about you from the start." The man who'd started out so conservative and soft-spoken had disappeared. His tone of voice stayed level, albeit heavy with some kind of controlled anger. "You could have stayed objective with David Crowe. You could have just called me on the phone. You could have just asked for my opinion or even my help. Get over yourself, Agent Rhodes. This isn't about you or me. This is about Scotty Erickson—and maybe more."

Lockhart's eyes twitched when he mentioned Scott, and in that flicker of concern, Caitlyn realized the man was right. It had nothing to do with her. Lockhart hadn't tried to intimidate her in any way, yet Agent Caitlyn Rhodes, ten-year FBI veteran, felt like a rookie again. Her motivations had never been called out before, and the fact that it was a near stranger doing it made things worse. That the stranger was a 20-year FBI veteran that had caught serial killers made it even worse. That his motivation of finding Scott Erickson had never wavered made her want to throw up. He was the only one with the right priorities, when it was her job to take point and to be better than that.

It felt like he stared at her for hours until his eyes finally dropped. "Listen, we're behind the eight-ball on this one. We're well past the first twenty-four or even forty-eight hours. The weather washed most of the he evidence away. This was reported as a missing person, sure, but bearing in mind all we've already found out, we need to start treating it like a kidnapping. It's better to think the worst and find out we were wrong than to do it the other way around, right?"

Caitlyn's face twitched. "Right. So…what do we do from here?"

"First, we put out an Amber alert on Scott. We'll get the kid's picture out there and hope for a concerned citizen's help. When we stopped for gas earlier, I called the Ericksons and asked their permission to search Scott's computer. My knowledge of computers is shamefully limited, to tell you the truth, but as soon as you showed up it became federal. I called an agent I know in Bemidji, and his office should be running through the files as we speak."

Lockhart had gone over, or at least around, Caitlyn's head—a brazen and disrespectful thing to do, but it was the right thing to do under the circumstances. Caitlyn held back her instinct to chastise his behavior and let out a sigh. "From now on, please tell me when you plan on doing your own investigating. Like you said, this is federal jurisdiction now."

Lockhart smiled warmly and for the first time, Caitlyn noticed that he actually was a very handsome man, though she still found him entirely annoying.

"Fair enough," he said.

"So, former Special Agent, what's the next move?" Caitlyn asked.

"Well, considering that we don't have much else to go on and that we are looking at another five hour drive, I don't know about you, but I'm starving. You know any good places to eat around here?"

CHAPTER 8

They had driven through Grand Marais without much notice on the way to the Witch Tree in Grand Portage. Now they were stopping there for dinner. It was almost seven at night and the town was quiet. Normally busy from spring to Labor Day, the northern Minnesota tourist destination sat quietly in their little bay of Lake Superior.

As they rolled through the postage-stamp downtown, still larger than Crayton, one restaurant caught Lockhart's eye.

"Why don't we eat there? I've seen Sven and Ole's Pizza bumper stickers all over the state."

"Nah," Rhodes said dismissively. "The pizza is good, but The Angry Trout is better."

"The Angry Trout?" Lockhart asked. "How very Minnesotan."

The Angry Trout Café sat on the edge of the Grand Marais bay, right next to the marina. It looked antiquated, like some old fish-and-chips joint out East. Agent Rhodes assured him he would like it and Lockhart didn't offer any argument.

Actually, he felt bad about their confrontation, and he knew he hadn't played it well. Even though her own motivations had obstructed her judgment, he realized he shouldn't have made such a show of it. It just felt good to feel like an agent again. *Maybe it was the suit*, he considered, fondling his perfectly knotted tie and glancing at himself in the rearview mirror.

The two sat down at a table against the back wall of windows that looked out into the bay. A few of the biggest seagulls Lockhart had ever seen still stood out on the breaker rocks. They weren't nearly as susceptible as he was to the brutal winds that had gotten worse since they'd arrived in town.

A young waitress came over to take their order. She had a dyed pink streak in her blonde hair. She wore pink horn-rimmed glasses and had a punk-rock feel about her.

"What's good?" Lockhart asked Agent Rhodes.

"Everything," she said without hesitation. She then looked up at the waitress, closing her menu, as if she had it memorized. "I'll have the garden salad with vinaigrette and a bowl of the Lake Superior chowder."

"Uh," Lockhart said, reading as fast as he could. "I'll have the fish and chips."

"Herring or cod?" the waitress asked.

"I'll try the herring."

"Good choice," the waitress said scribbling the order on her pad. "It'll be right up."

"Thanks," Caitlyn said as she handed over her menu. She looked at Lockhart. "I eat here every time I can. They are only open from May to mid-October, so this must be one of their last days. They serve organically- and sustainable foods, using wind-powered electricity. They even invest in the neighborhood economy by purchasing as much as they can from local providers."

Lockhart smiled. "Are you trying to get me to buy a franchise or something?"

Agent Rhodes blushed a little. "No. It's just nice to see that kind of thing, given the kind of work we do."

Lockhart nodded in agreement and Rhodes looked out the window. He felt like he was in junior high. Sure, Rhodes was attractive, though she tried hard to hide it. Then again, she was also a federal agent, so that would at least give them something to talk about."

But Lockhart could only think of one thing.

"Go ahead," he said. "Ask."

Agent Rhodes turned back from the window. To her credit, she didn't try to play dumb. "Okay, fine. Why were you transferred from being an active FBI special agent assigned to serial killers to police chief in Mayberry? They're what? About 700 people in your jurisdiction there?"

"639," Lockhart corrected. He chewed his lip a moment before he went on. "Regardless of the rumors, I don't really know why it happened. After I tracked down The Taker in Crayton, I got reassigned. The old chief of police, John Donaldson, died during the investigation. He was a good man."

"The Taker killed him? I thought he only killed kids."

"He did. Donaldson died of a heart attack in his sleep."

"So...?" Rhodes asked.

"So, the next thing I knew, some higher-ups had decided to reassign me."

Caitlyn shook her head. "That doesn't make sense. There has to be more to the story."

Lockhart shrugged. It was a thought that hadn't left his mind for over a month. "I'm sure there is, but for the life of me, I can't figure it out—not yet, at least."

The server brought their food and Lockhart was glad to find that Rhodes had been right. It all tasted fresh and homemade and delicious. The herring was tender with a crunchy cornmeal breading that warmed his stomach in ways he desperately needed.

Agent Rhodes's mood lightened as she ate and the silence returned, but only because they were otherwise focused. When they had both finished their respective meals, just as another awkward silence reared its head, Rhodes' phone rang.

"Rhodes," she answered. "Oh, really?" She looked at Lockhart as she spoke. "Can you send me the address? Great. Thanks, Agent."

She put her phone away and quickly said, "That was Bemidji. They did a check of Scott's computer. They said the order was from me."

Lockhart smiled.

"They were able to pull a regularly repeating IP address from a chat log," Rhodes said, standing up and flagging down the server.

"Where from?" Lockhart asked.

"Right here in Grand Marais. Can you believe that?"

"Agent Rhodes, give it enough time, and you will come to believe just about anything."

CHAPTER 9

Tanya Murphy paced back and forth in her room. Illuminated only hazily by the dancing glow of candles, her room was otherwise black: black paint on the walls, blackout blinds on the windows, and black sheets on her bed.

She paced and chewed the nubs of her black-polished nails as she took momentary glances at her computer screen, as if she could manifest a message, email or any other kind of response to appear by sheer force of will.

"Come on, Scott. Stop being such a jerk," she said to the computer screen. "I'm sorry, all right?"

A gentle knock tapped at her door. "Tanya?" her mother asked, the woman's voice muffled by the door and her blaring stereo.

Tanya ignored her, just as she did anyone who refused to refer to her as Shadow.

The knock came again, and her mother asked, "Tanya?" a little louder his time.

Tanya was in no mood to deal with her mom. She stomped to the door and yelled, "I told you! Don't call me…" She swung the door open and there stood her mother. Behind her was a middle-aged guy in a nice suit, along with a stuck up looking woman.

"Tanya," her mother said at a near whisper, "the FBI is here. What did you do?"

CHAPTER 10

Cleanliness is next to godliness, or so they say. If nothing else, cleanliness just makes sense. Not that long ago, doctors didn't even know germs existed, until research was done to figure out why midwives had such superior live child birth results.

Doctors didn't sterilize their instruments, wear gloves or masks, or even wash their hands, and they had no problem cutting right into a patient's heads in such a state. They also used ether, a horrible drug known to cause hallucinations. Until the 1960s, women were given ether, then strapped down during childbirth by doctors who claimed to know better than anyone else. The mothers-to-be would thrash and moan, in such a feral state that they later couldn't remember what they had done—or what the doctors had done to them, for that matter. It caused many to wonder, *How could anyone devote a life to such things?*

Over time, Louis Pasture, Alexander Fleming and Joseph Lister perfected their techniques and changed the world—and not only by bringing the classic mouthwash to so many bathroom sinks. Their goals stretched far beyond that of the average person, and they aimed for the good of the entire world.

The man called Vlad smiled to himself as he looked over his freshly sterilized instruments, admiring their history, their precision, and their capacity for perfection. Sadly, he had no such aspirations for the betterment of all mankind. His focus was...more specific.

While he abhorred the use of chemicals such as ether, he found it more than necessary to implement the usage of leather straps to keep people from thrashing around too much. A little bruising was far better than the alternative, as far as he was concerned.

As he stood over the boy, he dabbed the lad's brow with a cool rag. He was sweating horribly despite the cool air coming in through the open windows.

"Please! Please let me go," the boy begged.

There was no point in talking to the boy. Given his state of mind, Vlad was sure he'd never comprehend the importance of what was being done. He wanted to tell the boy that things could be worse, but in the context of the situation, his words would have more than likely fallen on deaf ears.

Really, it was all his little girlfriend's fault. If she had just followed instructions, none of it would have been necessary. *Well,* most *of it wouldn't have been necessary.*

He didn't break this sad news to the boy, but he did have one question that had to be asked. He stooped over the kid and said, "Out of curiosity, are you right- or left-handed?"

CHAPTER 11

Tanya Murphy sat across from Agent Rhodes and Chief Lockhart, her arms crossed in defiance.

Caitlyn felt sympathetic to the girl, for not so long ago, she'd been just like her. She'd never gone full goth, but that feeling of need for belonging was universal. Of course, back then the kids didn't carry laptops and tablets; some—and only a select privileged few—had pagers, and only of the numeric variety. Nevertheless, Caitlyn could relate to the blackness in Tanya's apparel and attitude.

The girl wore a scowl that was supposed to look intimidating, but it came across as just a weak front. It had turned into a staring contest, and neither Tanya nor Caitlyn was willing to flinch first. This left it to Lockhart to break the silence.

"You know, I met Marilyn Manson once." Lockhart said it casually, from his slouched posture in an overstuffed chair, as if he were just chatting in a bar.

Tanya kept up her icy veil and Agent Caitlyn Rhodes wondered where he was going with it.

"I was working in Chicago about ten years back when a bunch of bad stuff happened. Anyway, people found all these Marilyn Manson albums so naturally, we had to talk to him. It was nothing official, but still."

Lockhart must have said something to crack the ice because Tanya allowed a "So what?" to escape her lips.

"So," Lockhart continued, "he was questioned. That was weird in itself. He's a pretty tall guy and there he stood in a black leather corset and garter belt, right before a concert."

For a moment, Caitlyn thought she saw a smile on Tanya's face, but then the girl repeated her nonchalant and unimpressed "So?"

"I remember thinking it seemed like a stupid thing to ask him questions about a murder he didn't have anything to do with. He was just being judged because of the way he looked and the songs he wrote. It kinda goes against the whole freedom-of-expression thing, you know?"

Lockhart eyed Tanya for a second; he was a lot smoother than Caitlyn had expected.

"Being part of a crime, but only sort of. Maybe he didn't think anything of it, or maybe it was hard on him to think about what people had done. Maybe it ate away at him."

Tanya's lip quivered.

Lockhart had broken through without even mentioning Scott, playing it hard or anything else of the sort, and Caitlyn followed Lockhart's lead.

"Tanya..." Rhodes started.

The very mention of the girl's real name caused her face to immediately harden, and Shadow reverted to her steely gaze.

Caitlyn looked over at Lockhart who gave a subtle shake of his head.

"Her name's not Tanya," he said. "It's Shadow."

Tanya, aka Shadow, offered the I-told-you-so look of a spoiled child, as if her father had just taken her side in some playground dispute or sibling rivalry.

Lockhart was placating her and he did it very well.

"Shadow," he continued, "I don't want to play games. I'm not gonna treat you like you are stupid, or play good cop/bad cop. We need you to tell us about Drake."

Caitlyn was confused for a moment. She hadn't picked up until that moment that Lockhart was referring to their Internet identities—ones they probably lived out in real life, too.

"I-I don't know what you're talking about," Tanya mumbled.

Lockhart leaned forward. "We don't have time for you to play games with us either, Shadow. Drake is missing, and we found blood on the cliff."

Tanya started to open her mouth. She looked surprised, as if she desperately wanted to speak up but then her jaw snapped shut again.

Lockhart knew he was losing her, and Rhodes was growing angrier by the minute. Caitlyn wasn't interested in Tanya, or Shadow, or whatever the stubborn girl wanted to call herself. She was already sick of the girl's desire to be a hard case and fight the system. "You better start talking Tanya. I'd be well within my jurisdiction to arrest you for interfering in a federal investigation, and if you don't—"

Lockhart cut her off before she could finish the threat. "Don't waste your time, Agent Rhodes. She isn't going to talk and she knows we won't arrest a teen without concrete evidence that she was involved. Shadow here is one smart cookie, and she clearly doesn't give a damn about Scott."

Tanya's eyes burned fiercely at Lockhart as soon as he mentioned Scott, but she bit down on her lip and said nothing.

Lockhart leaned back in his chair with a look of both defeat and boredom.

"Personally, I think the kid was pretty pathetic. I remember guys like him in school. Even in my day, before all this Internet mumbo-jumbo, there were the guys who dreamt of sitting on our bench, wearing our helmets, and getting the girl and the glory. " He paused to shake his head.

"Instead, those idiots dressed up to look different, just to hide the fact that they were nothing but pathetic losers. I mean, come on! This Scott kid even came all the way from Crayton to drive you, what? Forty miles? How pathetic!—"

Tanya launched forward from her chair toward Lockhart faster than Caitlyn would have imagined she could, but Lockhart must have seen it coming.

He slid from his chair and stepped around the coffee table. Tanya ran into him and he wrapped his arms around her.

"Shut up! Shut up! Shut up!" she yelled in a high-pitched scream that quickly turned into a wailing sob.

Lockhart held her like a frightened child. Her face was buried into his chest as he quietly said, "Shhh, it's okay. I'm sorry. I'm sorry, Tanya..."

When the police chief looked over at Caitlyn, his eyes were filled with sorrow.

CHAPTER 12

Nothing about the world made sense. Holding a thought was impossible. The images that swirled around Scott's head blended together in a strange tapestry of colors and blurs. The sounds around him were just as confusing, like guttural moans with a metallic tweak.

He tried to move, to lift his arms and his legs, but he couldn't. His limbs were lead blocks. The only movement he could will at all was the rolling of his eyes in his head, and even that was difficult. There was no feeling in his arms or legs, and his heart raced at the thought. *Am I...paralyzed? Jesus!*

The thoughts tumbled around in his mind with such discord that all he could feel was an overwhelming panic. *Where is Tanya? What happened? How did I get here? Where am I?*

His missed his parents, and for just a moment, his wishful thinking tricked him into thinking he was still at home, snug in his bed, but caught in the middle of a bad dream. It reminded him of the time he'd had the flu as a little boy; back then, his parents always had that look on their face—*that* look. They'd kept promising him he'd be okay and reminding him how good God is, but their eyes betrayed them. They were afraid, and he knew it.

Now, he was afraid. At that moment, trapped wherever he was in that hellish nightmare, Scott was afraid and began to ponder all the evils he'd done in his life, no matter how small. *Have I really been that bad?* he thought. *Do I deserve...this?* He just couldn't get a handle on what was happening. The patterns of rust brown and gray danced with shadows, streaks of colors.

The spider tracks of a bead of sweat crept down

the side of Scott's face. He could only feel the slightest of tickles as it ran down the back of his neck and disappeared.

Spiders? Scott thought. *Are there spiders on me? Are bugs crawling on my arms and legs, little insects that I can't even feel? Am I...could I be still out at the Witch Tree?* He knew if he was, the wildlife would eventually overtake him. The ants, the mosquitoes, the little biting lady bugs, and the black flies would all come out and...

No, no, that can't be right. Not spiders, mosquitoes, or ants. It's almost winter, and the bugs are gone. That can't be bugs...can it? Wait...no, I can't be outside. I don't feel cold. I must be inside, where it's safe. Only he didn't feel safe.

It was a slight, gentle touch at first, the pressure of a feather that suddenly made Scott feel better. It was tender and caring as the pressure moved slowly across his forehead, dabbing at the sweat. A cool rag touched his face here and there, chasing away the spiders, just like his mother had done years ago to help break the fever.

"Mom..." Scott slowly tried to mutter, as if the word itself carried asylum for his swimming senses.

"No," replied the voice, as dark and jarring as it was familiar.

Scott's eyes swam in their sockets, trying to focus and make sense of the blended images. The face he finally focused on, as well as he could focus, didn't make sense. *Is that one face looking down at me—or two or three?* It was all so muddled. Scott had gotten drunk only once, and he had gotten so sick he'd sworn he'd never do it again, but this was even worse; it was as if he were drunk on a ship in the middle of stormy waters. Everything around him turned on its side as he slid farther and farther down the rabbit hole.

That face, or those faces, leaned in close to the side of his head. The sound was a whisper, but it boomed and echoed inside Scott's head. "It's better if you don't watch what's about to happen."

The words were almost sympathetic, but the tone was grave and cold...and very, very true.

CHAPTER 13

Crayton Police Chief Darren Lockhart waited inside the house with Tanya as Agent Rhodes went outside to make some phone calls. She was eager to get a sketch artist to Grand Marais and to search the database for the alias 'Vlad.'

Lockhart sat patiently as Tanya composed herself. The mascara around the girl's eyes had turned into perpetual black tears. "Tell me about that night," he said.

Tanya rolled her raccoon eyes, trying in vain to convey the body language of someone much colder and tougher than she actually was. "Drake…er, I mean, Scott, picked me up around eleven. We went out to the Witch Tree. We did the ceremony and we left."

"Who is 'we'? Did that include Scott?"

"No. It was just me and the other three girls. Vlad said the end of the ceremony involved the men and that we should leave, so we left."

"If Scott gave you a ride there, how did you get home?"

"I hitched a ride with Raven."

"So you *knew* someone else there besides Scott?" Lockhart asked as he scribbled down notes.

"Yeah," Tanya scoffed. "We got confirmed in church together. Her real name is Stephanie Makowski."

Lockhart jotted the name down, along with the girl's address and phone number, which Tanya retrieved from her cell phone and reluctantly handed over. "Did you know anyone else there?"

"No. Just Scott and Steph."

Lockhart raised an eyebrow. "What about Vlad?"

Tanya shifted in her seat. "Not really. I met him online, but we'd never met in person. He's cool. He just seemed to know stuff—like, he knew me."

Lockhart asked a few more questions about Vlad, none of which led anywhere, and then excused himself and went outside to converse with Agent Rhodes. Whoever Vlad was, he'd done well to cover his tracks and reveal almost nothing about himself—not even to Tanya, who was obviously one of his biggest fans.

Rhodes switched off her cell just as Lockhart stepped outside. "There's a local artist who works with police for sketches. She lives in Lutsen and can be here in about thirty minutes with the local police for an official statement."

"Good," Lockhart said, his eyes focused on nothing in particular.

Caitlyn looked at Lockhart inquisitively for a moment, her head tilted to the side. A gust of wind picked up, a single strand of blonde hair came undone from her ponytail. It fell gently across her face. Lockhart almost started to reach out to move it, but held himself in check.

"How did you do that in there?" Agent Rhodes asked.

"Do what?"

"How did you know how far to push that girl?"

Lockhart sighed as he sat down on the front cement step with a slight groan. His knees always hurt when winter was on the horizon. The temperature made it hard to want to get out and run, and he grew stiff easily without his morning jog. He glanced up at Agent Rhodes and explained, "I spent almost twenty

years tracking down murderers with the Bureau. You
and I know nine out of ten people can't do what we do.
Chasing after burglars, rapists, kidnappers, murderers—
it's a lot to handle. The big picture of a crime is too hard
for people to look at without blinking. The problem is, if
you look at the big picture too long, you forget about
the small stuff, like how to talk to people like they are
human beings instead of just potential victims or
suspects."

Caitlyn sat down next to him and pulled her coat
tight, releasing a small shiver. "Well, what about you?
Have you ever forgotten about the small stuff, Chief?"

Lockhart didn't answer right away. He could admit
his shortcomings, but that didn't mean he liked to think
about them. Finally, he turned his head and looked her
directly in the eyes. "Yeah, I did."

Agent Rhodes's eyes looked uncharacteristically
soft, even thoughtful. "What changed you?"

Lockhart reached into his coat pocket and pulled
out his Crayton PD badge. "I've learned more about
how to treat and talk to people in the last month than I
ever knew in all my years with the FBI. There's
something about small towns, I guess, that make you
take note of the small things."

Agent Rhodes smiled. "Were you really a football
player in high school?"

Lockhart shook his head slowly. "No, and I hated
what I just did in there. It just came down to the fact
that I knew her better than she thought I did."

Lockhart's phone rang, and he saw that it was his
mom. He stood up, excused himself from Agent Rhodes,
and walked off to the edge of the lawn. The wind blew
strongly, and he knew that would make talking on the
phone more difficult than if he had the house to block it

out, but he didn't feel like explaining his inevitable conversion and his mother's Alzheimer's to Rhodes. "Hi, Mom," he said, trying to raise his voice over the wind as he cupped his hand around the mouthpiece.

"Darren, is everything okay?" his mother asked, sounding concerned.

"Yeah, Mom. Why?"

"Oh, I can barely hear you. Is it windy there?"

"Yes, Mom. A little cold too."

"Well, I guess that's why they call it the Windy City."

Lockhart almost had to laugh when he realized his mother thought he was in Chicago. It was strange that she would have thought that of all the places he'd been stationed. He hadn't even thought of his time there for years, until he'd used it to help get through to Tanya. His mother saying it made him smile. *Maybe there is some order to all the chaos in the world, some rhyme and reason that goes beyond pure coincidence,* he humored to himself as he asked, "Is everything okay, mom?"

"Everything's great, Darren. I just wanted to call and let you know that your father and I checked into the hotel."

Lockhart let out a sigh of relief. "Thanks for calling, Mom. I hate to cut this short, but I'm in the middle of a case."

"Oh, don't let me stop you." There was a pause. "And Darren…"

"Yeah, Mom?"

"I just wanted to tell you how proud your father and I are of you and all the hard work you put in. That sort of thing gets remembered. There are big things in store for you, honey." He could hear her smile as she said it, and he was glad she was blissfully ignorant. He was glad that she didn't know how things really were. He was glad she didn't have to miss her husband.

"Thanks, Mom. Say hello to Dad for me. Love you."

Lockhart stood for a moment with cell phone still in hand. His mother was happy. The transfer had been hard on him, but hearing his mother excited instead of worried meant more to him than anything. After a moment, he turned and walked back to Agent Rhodes, who had busied herself playing with her smartphone.

She looked up. "Is everything okay?"

"Yup, fine. Thanks. What do you think? Time to go pay this Raven a visit?"

CHAPTER 14

In art of any form, as much as natural talent, the only real way to get better is through practice, consistency, and the ability to learn from mistakes. And, of course, there is patience.

A quiet and controlled working environment is preferable, if not mandatory. One with a view of the changing seasons is a bonus.

First, connect the radius and ulna bones using plates and screws. The use of screws on bones can create an unnerving sensation at first. The grinding nature of it all digs deep and creates that same feeling as fingernails on a chalkboard, except with screws...in bones.

Next, attach the arteries and veins using micro-vascular surgical techniques. Here is where the patience thing comes in, along with a steady hand.

If successful, the blood will start to flow through the arm. At that point, each muscle will need to be repaired individually. The tendons are fixed to tendons and tendons to muscle junctions.

After fixing the muscles at the back of the hand, it is time to fix the muscles and nerves in the palm of the hand. At this point, a severed nerve would be devastating to the procedure, as well as a difficult lesson to learn. The skin is then inspected.

It is then possible to repair the median, ulnar, and radial nerves.

Some finger motion might be possible immediately after surgery, but there is always the danger of tissue rejection—not to mention the psychological hazards.

CHAPTER 15

Adults are relatively easy to interview and interrogate, at least as far as legalities are concerned. Teens, on the other hand, are under the protection of their parents and cannot be questioned without a legal guardian present. This made things much more difficult for Lockhart and Rhodes, even under the best of situations.

Agent Caitlyn Rhodes had thought Tanya Murphy was difficult to deal with, but Raven was something different entirely. Compared to Raven, Tanya was an open book. Instead of cold, angry eyes, Raven's were sterile and empty. They were dark brown, set behind layers of black eye makeup. Disinterested wasn't the right word, but it was the only one Caitlyn could think of when she looked at the girl's empty expression. For all Caitlyn knew, Raven could have been stoned on drugs and probably was.

Caitlyn followed Lockhart's lead from earlier. "Raven, we are here to talk to you about your friend Shadow."

The girl's eyes remained blank. Her name might have been Raven, but her mother—perched over her shoulder—was a hawk. She was a thin WASP of a woman, dressed conservatively in a knee-length pink skirt suit reminiscent of Jackie Kennedy, and she stood with all the poise and posture of a soldier on guard duty. Mrs. Makowski hovered behind the chair in which Raven slouched, her hands set on the back of the chair on either side of her daughter's head, appropriately looming like a gargoyle over a gothic church. Lockhart had to play things pretty smooth just to convince her that they didn't need their lawyer present.

"Who's Shadow?" Raven asked obliviously.

"Your friend, Tanya Murphy," Caitlyn answered.

Raven gave a condescending glare and scoffed. "That bitch isn't my *friend*."

Caitlyn looked up at Raven's mother and expected some kind of comment on her daughter's language, but no such scolding came. "Regardless," Caitlyn continued, "Tanya told us you were with her two nights ago at the Witch Tree. She said you gave her a ride home."

"Impossible. My daughter was at home with me two nights ago," Mrs. Makowski chimed in.

Raven gave a triumphant smirk without breaking eye contact with Agent Rhodes. It was bad enough to have a parent answer questions for their child, but an answer that contradicted an earlier statement made things even worse. Even if it was a lie, it was an alibi.

Caitlyn didn't know how far she could go with the mother, but Lockhart didn't seem interested in the mom. He simply sat there casually, looking over his notes and jotting things down. It didn't even look like he was paying attention. "Why 'Raven'?" he asked without looking up from his notepad.

"What?" Raven asked. Her voice cracked for a moment, and he'd clearly caught her off guard with the change of subject.

"I get Shadow. It's all dark and creepy. I get Vlad because of the vampire thing. But why Raven? Are you a football fan?" If Lockhart was just playing dumb, he was pretty convincing about it.

Raven sat up with a sneer that overflowed with contempt. "Because I'm 'doubting dreams no mortal ever dared dream before.'" She leaned back into her chair smugly, as if she had just proven a point.

It was finally time for Caitlyn to act superior. "I

think you mean 'doubting, *dreaming* dreams no mortal ever dared *to* dream before.'"

Both Raven and Lockhart stared at Caitlyn. Lockhart looked impressed, while Raven balled up her tiny, stark-white hands.

Lockhart shook his head. "Hmm. I don't remember that part in *The Simpsons* episode I saw. Still, it doesn't answer the question. Why a poem that a lot of people evidently know? Or, in your case, *sort of* know. Why not something darker, more unique? I mean, 'Vlad' is a lot cooler than some bird."

Raven bit her lip, and Lockhart set his eyes on her. He stared right through her, and Raven looked helpless for just a moment. She didn't have a smart remark to shoot back at him, and she was clearly struggling to hold in whatever she wanted to say in response.

"Why do you keep talking about this Vlad character?" her mother asked.

Lockhart didn't flinch and continued to stare Raven down. "No reason. Just an example I heard once." He looked up at Mrs. Makowski. "Then again, the more I say it, the dumber it gets. I mean, can you imagine a grown man going around calling himself that? *Vlad*?" Lockhart chuckled, and even Mrs. Makowski let out a little snicker.

Raven's nostrils flared, and her teeth gnashed together, as if they'd insulted the love of her life.

Caitlyn saw it immediately. "Is something wrong, Raven?"

Raven bit down on her lower lip hard enough to leave an impression in the skin, but she still said nothing.

Lockhart braced his hands on the arms of the chair and pushed himself to his feet. "Well, I guess that's all we have. Thank you for your time, Mrs. Makowski." He put out his hand, and Raven's mom shook it limply.

"You know, Mr. Lockhart, it was out of courtesy to law enforcement that I allowed you in my home and to question my daughter, but what answers were you looking for?"

Lockhart dug a card out of his jacket pocket and handed it to her. "Oh, didn't I say? A teenage boy your daughter might know went missing two days ago at the Witch Tree. We're doing our best to get answers for his mom and dad, but it isn't looking good." He didn't dwell on the point for even a second. Instead, he turned to the door. "Well, have a good night, ladies. Hope it's not a 'midnight dreary,'" he said, returning a blank glance at Raven, who only rolled her eyes at him.

CHAPTER 16

Lockhart wasn't even able to reach the car before Agent Caitlyn Rhodes asked, "What the hell was that? We were getting somewhere."

Lockhart turned. Rhodes looked upset, or at least confused, but he understood why. He hadn't exactly been forthright about how he was going to play the interviews. "Really? It didn't seem that way to me."

"She would have cracked. When you pushed about Vlad, she wanted to say something." Rhodes clicked the auto-unlock button on her car keys.

Lockhart climbed into the passenger side. With the sun long since set, it was getting colder outside, and he rubbed his hands together for warmth. "Maybe, but her mom got in the way. She was on the defensive from the get-go. If we'd have pushed too hard, it would have been over. As soon as she answered for her daughter, our side of the questioning was basically done. Never make accusations in front of an overbearing parent. They'll lie just to prove you wrong. Now, at least there's a seed of doubt for the next time we talk to her dark little songbird."

Caitlyn turned on the car and sat there for a moment in park. Lockhart wasn't sure if she was thinking about how much she agreed with him or how much she disliked him, though neither would have surprised him. "Next time?" she finally asked.

"We aren't done with her," Lockhart said with a wry look.

Rhodes shifted the car into reverse and backed down the driveway. The dashboard clock said it was eight thirty p.m. It would be nearly two in the morning by the time he got home, and that was only if they left right away.

Lockhart wasn't much in the mood to spend another five hours in the car, and he was relatively certain Rhodes wasn't either. "Wanna get a room?" he asked. He hadn't intended the double-entendre, but that was exactly how it came out.

"Excuse me?"

"Do you want to get a room for the night? It's a long drive back to Crayton, or Duluth for that matter."

Agent Rhodes slowed the car to a stop just north of downtown Grand Marais and clenched her jaw to suppress a yawn. "You mean *rooms*, right? As in *separate* rooms?" she asked.

Lockhart smirked just slightly. "Of course. What did you think I meant?"

"Never mind," she said and rolled her eyes at him, something that Lockhart seemed to bring out in women as of late.

CHAPTER 17

Rhodes couldn't sleep that night. She just lay in her bed at the Harbor Inn in Grand Marais and stared at the ceiling. Her eyes floated around the room from the obligatory landscape paintings by local artists to the wicker chair and coffee table that sat next to the bed.

Slowly, she pulled herself up out of bed and decided to go out to get some fresh air, hoping a little walk would allow her mind to relax. Her room in the quaint hotel was actually located right on the Grand Marais main street.

Immediately she heard the cackling sounds of laughter and conversation nearby. Just a block down was a rooftop bar on top of the Gun Flint Tavern. Rhodes opted for a sense of community, reasoning that a nightcap could help things. *Maybe just being around normal people will be just what the doctor ordered,* she hoped. *Besides, a drink or two will take the edge off.*

It looked like the sum total of the Grand Marais night life was there: a few dozen late-season tourists enjoying the cool night and more than a few cocktails to warm their chilly bones. Rhodes wasn't much for drinking or hanging out in bars, but sitting alone in her hotel room wasn't doing her any good.

As Caitlyn walked up to the tiki-style bar, she paused. There, almost as if mocking her, sat Chief Lockhart. He back was turned, and there was no way he could have known she would show up there, but still, his presence suggested some kind of joke, as if she couldn't be trusted to do anything without him leading the way.

He had been cordial enough at lunch, but Rhodes had looked over her notes and thought about the earlier interviews, and his behavior had started to grate on her. She was a more-than-competent agent, and she had spearheaded the investigation. Without her, he wouldn't have even been part of it. Nevertheless, Caitlyn opted to swallow her pride, reflexively checking her hair and straightening her clothes before walking up to the bar next to him. "What's good here?" she asked and immediately regretted for the sophomoric sound of it.

Lockhart twisted his head to the side with no look of surprise. "Agent Rhodes. Out for a nightcap, huh?"

"As are you," she noted. Again, she felt strangely awkward all of the sudden. Social settings were far from her forte.

"Couldn't sleep. I think I'm too used to how Joy makes the beds at the B-and-B. Have a seat and take a load off."

Caitlyn thanked him and sat down. "So, what *is* good here?" she asked, motioning to the beer in front of Lockhart.

"Surly Furious." Lockhart looked up at the bartender. "That's right, isn't it, Marcus?"

The bartender nodded his head. "Yup. Sure is."

"Not sure how much of a beer-drinker you are, but Marcus says Schell's is good too—local stuff and all that. I'm more of a Nordeast guy, but…" He looked over at the beer taps. "Schell's Lite for the lady?"

Caitlyn wasn't much of a drinker, beer or otherwise, but she nodded.

The two sat quietly, neither seeming to know what to ask.

"Are you off the clock?" Lockhart finally asked.

"What do you mean?" Caitlyn said, doing her best not to show her disinterest in the taste of the beer she was nursing.

"Well, I wanted to ask you a personal question, but I wasn't sure if I was just talking to a woman in a bar or a federal agent."

The mention of federal agent incited the bartender to look across the bar in surprise at Rhodes, who smiled in return.

She played it safe. "How about you ask the question, and then I'll decide if I'm on the clock?"

Lockhart took another pull off his beer. "Fair enough. Why the FBI?"

"What's that supposed to mean?"

Lockhart lolled his head from shoulder to shoulder. "You were Dallas PD, right? I spent a little time in Dallas. There's more than enough to do around there for the locals. Seems like going through FBI training was a lot of work just to get assigned to a city fairly sleepy in comparison."

Caitlyn took another sip of her beer as she thought about how to respond. *Should I explain my father's expectations, considering he wanted a son? Should I tell him about the politics I had to deal with in Dallas to prove my desire to rise above? Should I tell him anything at all?* "It's not as sleepy as you think. There's plenty to do with the Canadian border, Native American land, and all the wonderful little foibles that people are prone to do anywhere else in the country."

Lockhart looked over at her. It was an innocent look, but it felt probing, as if he were trying to look inside her for the real motivation.

But Agent Rhodes was not one to be interrogated by anyone. "It's not like my reasons are any different from anyone else's. I mean, why did *you* join the Bureau? I mean—"

Lockhart saved her from having to backtrack. "Dad was military, and I came from a family of all boys. Maybe too much testosterone or expectations or something. Who knows? Pick your psychoanalytical explanation." Lockhart drained the rest of his glass and set it on the bar, motioning for another. "Of course, I have to admit I also liked being top dog. I liked the authority and control. Seemed to suit me, at least until recently."

Rhodes wasn't sure how to respond to such an admission. She felt as though anything she could have said would just come out as condescending. Instead, she just sat there and finished her beer, then informed her drinking partner, "I plan on heading out at six."

Lockhart looked at his watch and saw that it was nearly midnight. "I'll be ready."

Rhodes stood up and excused herself for the night. Lockhart didn't say anything in response; he had clearly taken a turn with the conversation and Caitlyn figured it best to leave him to his own thoughts.

Rhodes walked slowly down the empty city streets. The sounds from the bar quickly thinned as the patrons wandered or stumbled back to their hotel rooms for the night. A frigid wind blew in off the bay, and Rhodes couldn't help but think of Chief Lockhart sitting alone on the barstool.

CHAPTER 18

It wasn't until after noon the next day that Agent Caitlyn Rhodes dropped Chief Lockhart off in Crayton. Rhodes informed him that she would be at the Bemidji FBI office to do some follow-up work. The five-hour drive from Grand Marais left little to be desired, and she said she needed to get some work done. The thirty minutes to the Bemidji office was no doubt far more appealing than another two hours back to Duluth.

Lockhart bid her goodbye with a small feeling of regret. He had hoped to glean more from questioning Raven and Shadow, but with no better leads, both he and Rhodes had other duties that required their respective attention.

For Lockhart, that meant his weekly visit to Mrs. Edelstein's house at the edge of town to listen to how she thought the world was going to "H-E-double-hockey sticks," then to the City Council meeting in the K-12 school gymnasium.

With a heavy heart, Lockhart switched out of his suit and back into his dreaded police uniform. He took a moment to look at himself in the mirror. The man who looked back didn't appear too excited to be there.

At the five p.m. City Council meeting, Lockhart preoccupied himself by searching for and uploading Genesis songs while he attempted to balance on just the back two legs of his chair.

Lockhart got a text just as the meeting reached a rather heated debate over funding for the filling of potholes. According to the text from Deputy Lind, Justin Erickson's truck had been found in the woods five miles outside of Crayton.

Lockhart didn't need directions to the scene. Just

as Freddie said, the truck was five miles out of town—*exactly* five miles. It just sat there, somewhat at an angle with the road, as if it had been ditched, but not so far off the road that someone had lost control of it. There were no skid marks to suggest a quick stop, and the doors were closed.

Deputy Lind sauntered up to Lockhart's police cruiser with a pleasant grin on his face. "Afternoon, Chief," he said with a nod. Admittedly, Freddie didn't exactly cut a swath of intimidation as far as authority figures were concerned, but he was a solid officer and one hell of a good cook. Beneath his skinny, grill-burned arms and almost-awkward, loping gait, Freddie had an edge to him that, if nothing else, would make for a good backup in a bar brawl.

"Afternoon Freddie," Lockhart said as he pulled himself out of his police cruiser. His shoes crunched into the loose rock on the side of the road. "Who found the truck?"

"I did actually. I was headin' over to Blackduck to pick up a couple things when I saw it just parked there."

Lockhart stared at the truck with a cocked head. He resisted the temptation to go over and get a closer look, not wanting to risk that the scene would be disturbed. "Have you been inside the cab?"

Freddie shook his head. "Nope. I took a peek to see if anyone was in there, touched the hood to see if the engine was still warm—and don't worry, I used a glove—but that's it. Cab was empty, engine was cold. I figured that since the Feds are involved, it'd probably be best not to touch anything." He gave Lockhart a wink. Freddie had learned his lesson about crime scenes the first time he and Lockhart had met.

The chief patted his deputy on the shoulder.

"You've come a long way in a short time, Deputy. Did you call Bemidji?"

"Sure did. That lady agent should be here anytime with their lab techs." Freddie eyed Lockhart for a moment. "Tell you what, there are worse sites to see. I heard Agent Rhodes ain't too hard on the eyes."

Lockhart couldn't help but give Freddie a small smirk. He wasn't interested in going down that road with him, but there was no harm in letting Freddie be Freddie. Still, he couldn't resist goading him a little. "How's the fiancée doing Freddie?"

Deputy Lind snorted. "You're no fun."

"So they tell me, Deputy. Go grab your camera and start documenting the scene."

Freddie's face slid into a look of concern. "You think we'll find Scotty, Chief?"

Lockhart's eyes traced along the length of the truck. "I hope so Freddie. I truly hope so."

CHAPTER 19

Agent Caitlyn Rhodes hadn't expected to be back in Crayton so soon. She had been in the middle of filing her report and sending in an expense report for her hotel room in Grand Marais when she got the call from Deputy Lind in Crayton to let her know Erickson's truck had been found.

When she arrived at the truck with crime scene investigators, she was surprised to see that both Chief Lockhart and Deputy Lind were there just waiting. Lockhart was seated on the trunk of the police cruise, and Lind was leaning on the side of the car. "Is there any reason that you two haven't marked off the area?" Caitlyn asked, pointing the investigators to the truck and outlining the specifics she wanted to see.

"No reason to," Lockhart said as he hopped off the hood to greet her. "This isn't a crime scene. Technically, it's just an abandoned vehicle. Plus, this road hardly gets used this time of day, so traffic is easy to reroute without making a scene of it."

"Is that all?" Caitlyn asked, her annoyance rising.

"No. There is also the fact that this is *your* investigation, and I'm not about to wander around the scene and mess anything up. This is your show."

Caitlyn listened to him say the words, but she wasn't sure how much *he* believed them. He was a good investigator and an excellent interrogator. Not only that, but he knew it. She got the feeling his cooperation only went so far—as long as she was handling things the way he would if he were in her place. It was incredibly condescending, no matter how nicely he tried to do it.

The CSI went to work taking photographs of the

area. They dusted the truck for prints inside and out and checked for stray hairs or fibers. They sprayed it down and checked it for blood or other bodily fluid stains with an ultraviolet light. They were as thorough as possible, all under the watchful eye of Agent Rhodes.

One investigator brought a plastic bag over to Caitlyn. In it was a pink parking citation. She turned it over in her hands and read the date. It had been issued the day after Scott's supposed disappearance, but before the missing persons report was filed.

Lockhart and Lind took it upon themselves to look over her shoulder. Lockhart asked, "Why didn't this shoot up about a dozen red flags in the system?"

Caitlyn shook her head. "This ticket was cited just outside of Grand Marais. There are a few departments in the upper part of the state that still write out parking tickets by hand. There is a chance it wasn't officially filed yet."

Caitlyn turned to face the two men and saw that Lockhart's brow looked worried as he ground his teeth against his lower lip. "Great," he said without releasing his bite.

Caitlyn gave the bag back to the investigator as he finished up his search. Eventually, Caitlyn and the two officers were able to check out the truck for themselves. Nothing seemed to be out of place at all. Lockhart climbed into the driver seat and noted that he and Scott were about the same height. The seat and mirror positions all seemed to match up with the dimensions. Forensics had pulled prints off the steering wheel, gear shift, and driver side door handle, but it could take days to get a hit on them, assuming that the prints weren't those of Scotty or his parents and that they were in the system to begin with. The real goal was to pull matching prints off the parking ticket, and only time would tell if that could be accomplished.

"I don't get it," Deputy Lind said as he slammed the passenger door shut. "If Scott drove this truck back here, where is he? There aren't any footprints in the dirt around the truck, so he surely didn't run off into the woods. Do you think I should get old Tom Cooper's bloodhounds out here to see if they can't pick up a scent?"

Lockhart paced a bit, and Caitlyn thought she saw him snarl slightly. "No. I don't think that's going to result in anything other than listening to Tom explain why the Vikings won't ever win a Super Bowl."

"What did the parents say when you contacted them about the truck?" Caitlyn asked.

Lockhart stopped his pacing and glanced over at Freddie, then to back to Caitlyn. "We haven't talked to them about this yet."

"Are you kidding? So for all you know, Scott is at home right now, and we've been out here investigating a truck for no reason?" It seemed to Caitlyn that every time she thought she understood how Lockhart thought, he would do something to completely contradict himself.

"We tried earlier," Lockhart said. "The line was busy. We'd have tried again, but we wanted to see what the scene turned up. We didn't want to risk giving the family false hope."

Caitlyn conceded the point but still wanted to go talk with the parents. First, she called the FBI Motor Vehicle Division to see if they could get warrants to check street-level traffic cameras on the chance they might have caught something. "Do you have a photo printer in your office?" she asked Lockhart.

Lockhart looked surprised and confused. "Yeah. Why?"

"We might be missing something," Agent Rhodes said plainly.

Lockhart's eyes showed that he'd come to the conclusion that she was going to go talk to the parents with or without his consent. "What could they possibly see in a set of truck pictures?" he asked skeptically.

For the first time, Chief Lockhart didn't strike her as a federal agent, but it had nothing to do with the lackluster, ill-fitting uniform. He held back. He knew he should have been pressing for leads. He was already getting soft.

"We won't know until we ask, will we?" she asked.

As they sat in the Ericksons' living room, Lockhart stared at Caitlyn with a look of grinding contempt. His jaw was clenched, and he didn't move his eyes from her, even when he sat down at the long, polished dining room table.

Caitlyn spread the photos out in front of the Ericksons on their coffee table after she explained that their truck had been found just outside of town. Unfortunately, neither the Ericksons nor anyone else had seen hide nor hair of Scott since his disappearance had been reported.

"Please take a look at these pictures, Mr. and Mrs. Erickson. I know it's difficult, but can you tell me if anything seems out of place? Anything at all?"

Jessica Erickson looked off to the side of the pictures, and Justin scanned them for just a moment before he shook his head and pushed the photos back across the table. "That's my truck, all right," he said, "but nothin' looks wrong with it."

They had barely taken the time to look them over, but Caitlyn knew there had to be something they were missing. "Please, Mr. and Mrs. Erickson, if you can just look at these a moment longer. Please look at them very closely. Even the slightest detail might be helpful."

Jess didn't move her eyes from the table. "My husband says he doesn't see anything. Why are you wasting time showing us pictures of our truck when you could be out there doing something—anything—to find our son?"

"Mrs. Erickson, please—" Caitlyn started to say

But Chief Lockhart, whose gaze hadn't stopped burning into her, interrupted. "We're done here." He turned to the Ericksons with a gentle gaze. "Jess, Justin, I'm sorry to have interrupted your night." Then Lockhart walked over to the table and started to pick up the pictures.

Caitlyn grabbed his wrist, and Lockhart slammed his gaze against her again—this time with all the ferocity of a caged bear. His eyes were dark and heavy, as if he carried the weight of the world inside himself. She felt as though he were several feet taller than her and every bit as intimidating.

"They aren't done," Caitlyn said in a lowered voice, as if the Ericksons wouldn't be able to hear it.

Lockhart leaned in. "Yes they are."

"Wait," Justin said, just as it felt like Lockhart was going to snap. "I mean, I'm sure it's nothing, but..."

Lockhart turned away from Caitlyn and addressed Mr. Erickson. "What is it, Justin?"

"It's just...well, the trailer hitch."

Caitlyn looked down at the picture on the coffee table, and Justin spun it to face her and the chief. "What about it?" she asked.

"Well, we just bought it. It was perfectly polished chrome. Now it's all scratched up, like from a tow hitch. We haven't used it to tow anything yet."

Lockhart walked several paces ahead of Rhodes. He hadn't spoken since leaving the house. He was in a huff, and Caitlyn couldn't help enjoying it a little. He had been in control of the entire investigation, whether he meant to or not, and Caitlyn felt a small twinge of pride in showing that she wasn't just one of the sheep who would mindlessly follow his lead.

Agent Rhodes couldn't contain the "You don't have to say it" that escaped her lips in a moment of weakness, but she immediately regretted it.

Lockhart spun quickly before he reached the car. "That's the best thing you can think of to say right now? I told you so?" He turned back around, shaking his head, and got into the police cruiser.

Caitlyn stood there as Lockhart sat in the car with the engine idling. She stood there for over a minute, not knowing what his problem was, before he swung the door open and approached her again. She cut him off before he could speak. "What's your problem with me? I just uncovered new information on the case. How about you just admit that you were wrong about them not knowing anything?"

Lockhart's face scrunched up in a strange mix of a sneer and grimace. "New information? Tell me, Agent, how time sensitive was that intel, huh? Are you going to go track down that scuffed-knob lead tonight?"

"We wouldn't have known if we hadn't taken the time to ask," Caitlyn said defensively.

"And nine at night is the best time for that? Did you even bother to look at their faces? Jess probably hasn't slept in days. So at night, when they would be *blessed* with the reprieve of sleep, you figured a picture show of a dead end was the right thing to do? Can you even comprehend what those two are going through?"

Caitlyn said nothing by way of response.

Lockhart turned away and walked back to the car. Just before he grabbed the handle, he paused. His head was down, and his eyes were closed. Lockhart looked over his shoulder. "Let me tell you what they are going through." He turned his body to face her, his face empty. "At night, when all the lights are off, every sound makes them think their Scotty has come home. They imagine the sound of the doorknob turning, the floor squeaking with his footsteps, or—until tonight— the truck engine shutting off in the driveway. All they do is stare into the darkness and imagine that Scott is home, only to be disappointed over and over again."

Still, Caitlyn didn't say a word.

Lockhart's eyes dropped down and away. "Sure, your position gives you the authority and the right to question them, but being human should have been more important. I hope it was worth it. I really do."

CHAPTER 20

Police Chief Darren Lockhart wasn't able to sleep that night. Agent Caitlyn Rhodes decided to drive into Bemidji to get a hotel room and follow up on the forensic evidence from the Ericksons' truck.

He lay in his room at the bed-and-breakfast run by the police receptionist Joy and her sister Jill. Normally, he felt swaddled in the floral-print sheets and hand-sewn quilt, but not that night. That night, Lockhart needed something a little stronger to warm him; he needed a drink.

Around midnight, Lockhart walked through the door of The Pit Stop bar and sidled up to the bartender, Trevor, his feet crunching across discarded peanut shells on his way. Crayton had two bars, but Izzy's was better suited for watching sports and grabbing some buffalo wings. The Pit Stop was where Lockhart went when he just wanted to have a drink.

As Lockhart sat down on the faded, torn leather barstool, Trevor looked up from the glasses he was washing. It was a quiet night, and only two other people were there, seated at a table near the front windows.

"Havin' the usual, Chief?" Trevor asked, as if Lockhart ever drank anything else. The bartender's muscular arms flexed for a moment as he leaned on the bar. The uniform policy at The Pit Stop didn't include a requirement for sleeves, and Trevor took full advantage of that; however, when asked, the bartender would argue that he technically did have sleeves. They were just made of ink instead of fabric, and he couldn't take them off.

Trevor pulled a frosted beer mug out of the cooler and set it under the beer taps. He pulled the Grain Belt

Nordeast draw and filled the glass with a golden cascade of malted hops. He then set the full mug in front of Lockhart with a perfect head of foam on it and set a shot glass next to the coaster like a tagalong brother, never too far away. Trevor filled the shot with White Label Bushmills whiskey and pushed it toward the chief of police. Grain Belt and Bushmills was Lockhart's usual—his only.

Lockhart didn't hesitate. He took the shot down. After all, he'd been thinking about it for over an hour, but he didn't follow it up with his customary chase of beer and just let the shot burn in his mouth and throat.

Trevor looked up from drying glasses with his bar towel. "Anything wrong, Chief?" Trevor was normally a pretty quiet guy and never one to show so much as voluntary interest in people's private lives. Lockhart must have made it obvious, but he wasn't one to heap it on anyone's shoulders, bartender or otherwise.

"Yeah," Lockhart answered, "but it's nothing another shot can't solve."

Trevor gave a satisfied, if not ambivalent nod and refilled Lockhart's shot glass.

Darren Lockhart wanted to wallow a little. It was hard enough to get used to being a small-town cop without bumping into federal jurisdiction issues. The irony was not lost on him, but it made the whole thing all the more bitter.

He drummed his fingers on the chipped, water-marked mahogany bar as he stared at his slowly disappearing mug of beer. He hated losing his temper, but Agent Rhodes had pushed the family too hard. They were parents who'd lost a son and were hanging on by threads of hope that Scott was out there to be found and brought home. Rhodes uncovering the scuffs on the hitch meant nothing out of context and only served to further confuse the Ericksons.

Lockhart knew how they felt. Before his mother had been diagnosed with Alzheimer's, she'd wandered off one day. Lockhart had been on duty and hadn't even noticed that she wasn't making her usual semi-daily calls. It took three days to finally find her, and by the time they did, she was over 300 miles away. He knew the fear and panic of losing someone, but he also knew the relief in finding them. The Ericksons didn't yet have that luxury, and Lockhart desperately wanted to provide the relief for them somehow.

Lockhart hung around The Pit Stop for another hour before Trevor announced last call. Mid-pour of his third beer, Lockhart's phone rang; it was Agent Rhodes. Lockhart wondered aloud if she ever slept. "Lockhart," he said, less than enthusiastically.

"Chief Lockhart," Agent Rhodes's voice sounded official, as it had when they'd first met, "we have a hit on the fingerprints off the parking ticket."

Lockhart felt his stomach clench and churn slightly with a whirlpool of swirling alcohol and repression as he waited to hear who the prints belonged to. "Who?" he said, barely able to get the question out.

"Your missing person, Scott Erickson."

CHAPTER 21

Agent Rhodes waited as Chief Lockhart and Deputy Lind drained a pot of coffee between their respective gullets. When she had called him, Lockhart had admitted to drinking and said he wouldn't be able to make the drive to Bemidji. She made no attempt to show her distaste for his inebriated state, but she made sure to note that it was the second time in as many days that Lockhart had spent his off hours drinking.

Caitlyn was in no mood to make another trip to Crayton. She was still put off by the talking-down she'd received from Lockhart outside of the Ericksons' house earlier that night. Besides, the information was sensitive, and she needed federal resources to access it.

Both the chief and deputy looked exhausted. Caitlyn almost felt bad for the deputy for having to play designated driver from Crayton to Bemidji for his boss, but she had bigger things to worry about than their interrupted sleep patterns. She needed some answers, and she couldn't understand why Lockhart didn't seem to be treating the situation with the same urgency.

"Tell me," she started, "why are Scott Erickson's prints even in the system? He has no criminal record."

Lockhart shrugged, his eyes blurry with fatigue and his fading buzz. "How should I know?" he asked, his voice rife with disinterest.

"Actually," Deputy Lind said awkwardly, "I think I can answer that."

Both Caitlyn and Lockhart, who looked just as confused as she felt, turned their attention to the deputy; in turn, he looked down to the floor.

Lockhart started, sounding like a scolding father, "Freddie, why are Scott's prints in the system?"

Lind shifted his feet and played with his coffee mug. "Actually, most of the town is in the system."

It was Caitlyn's turn for less-controlled outrage. "Deputy Lind, if any of these prints were obtained illegally—"

The deputy instantly cut her off, and Caitlyn was somewhat glad; she really wasn't sure where she would have gone with such a threat.

"It's not illegal! Then again, I guess it's just not entirely legal either. Every year the local Boy and Girl Scout troops take a tour of the police station. We show them the cell, let them run the car sirens, and—"

"And *fingerprint* them?" Lockhart asked.

Freddie nodded. "Yeah. The kids think it's fun and all to get ink on their hands. We used to do just one or two kids to show them that everyone has different spiral patterns on their fingers. I guess about twenty years ago, Chief Donaldson got the idea to print 'em all—you know, just in case."

Lockhart stood up and walked over to the office window, his reflection upset and embarrassed. "Jesus Freddie... "

Caitlyn was concerned. Besides the civil rights violations, she knew those prints would never hold up in court.

"It's not like we ever really use 'em," Lind said in his defense. "We just keep 'em as a reference—you know, in case some kid spray-paints the water tower and leaves the can behind. We don't arrest him. We just keep an eye on him."

"Chief Lockhart, how many people are in your town?" Caitlyn asked, knowing full well that she had asked before, but for some reason, she couldn't currently remember.

"Latest count says 639, give or take."

Caitlyn turned to Lind. "And how many of those 639 do you have prints for?"

Deputy Lind paused for a moment to think. Caitlyn saw his long, thin fingers twitching, as though he were trying to calculate on them without her seeing. "Uh, legal and otherwise, somewhere just north of 500. Lots of people go into Scouts around here. Not much else for kids to do, I guess."

Caitlyn turned to Lockhart. "Are you planning on saying anything, or should I go over what I *could* be charging him with?"

Lockhart sat down on the edge of one of the desktops. His hands braced at his sides, and he allowed his legs to dangle and swing. "Freddie...what the hell, man?" And that was it.

Caitlyn waited for some kind of speech or at least some harsh words. He seemed to have little to no problem telling her what she had done wrong with the Ericksons, but evidently, his own deputy was immune to punishment. "Is that seriously all?" Caitlyn asked in disbelief after several moments of waiting.

Lockhart turned toward her. "What more do you want? My predecessor had a tenuous grasp on the law and poor judgment. If anything, it gave us an answer. That still doesn't change the result."

"What result?" Deputy Lind asked, looking utterly confused.

Caitlyn wanted to avoid the answer. She had hoped it was all a mistake, but by Lind's own admission, the prints were no doubt those of Scott Erickson. "If Scott's fingerprints were on a ticket the day *after* the supposed abduction, he *wasn't* abducted—and he certainly wasn't killed. The oils from the prints would have shown up different after testing. No point in planting prints on something if you're looking for a ransom or attempt blackmail. Still, the fingerprints could have been planted," Caitlyn suggested.

"On the ticket, the steering wheel, the door handle, *and* the gear shift? With no smudges from someone else driving with gloves on?" Lockhart countered.

"And why return the truck and disappear again?" Lind asked.

Caitlyn felt deflated, but she offered up all the possibilities she could think of. "Could've been remorse. He wanted to run off, but he felt bad about taking his dad's truck. Or, maybe he realized we'd be on the lookout for the plates and make. Who knows?"

"So what? That's it?" Lind asked, his voice desperate and edgy.

Lockhart stood slowly from his spot on the desk. He walked over and put a hand on Lind's shoulder. "Not much we can do. The FBI involvement is over since he was alive *after* the supposed crime. There have been no ransom or other demands, so we can't assume it was an abduction. All we can do is keep the missing persons report open and hope he contacts us at some point."

Lind looked like he had something to say, but instead he turned and stomped out the door, slamming it behind him.

Lockhart looked at Caitlyn. His eyes were averted for a moment before he looked up to speak. His eyes hung on his face like an exhausted, desperate rock climber near falling. His face was covered in gray whiskers. He also started to say something but stopped himself. His face lightened. "Good luck with your investigation, Agent Rhodes. I wish I could have done more to help."

With that, he put out his hand, and Caitlyn shook it in quiet resignation. It hadn't been the best couple of days, and she wasn't really sure what to think of Lockhart as a man. As an investigator, he had great instincts, but he had a blind spot when it came to his little corner of the world, that tiny little excuse of a town where he wore that despicable uniform and made his home in a bed-and-breakfast. "Thanks, Chief Lockhart. I appreciate your help."

Lockhart smirked. "Darren. My name is Darren." After the casual introduction to his first name, he turned and walked to the door, but then he offered one last turnaround. "Gimme a call if you ever need a hand."

CHAPTER 22

Anyone with any sense heading up the North Shore on Highway 61 stopped in at Betty's Pies. A while back, the place had been little more than a white-boarded lean-to off the highway. Times had changed, though, and money had come in. Not only had they built a larger restaurant just up the hill, but they'd even branched out to locations in the Twin Cities.

Still, it was the original Betty's Pies that did it best. Some people swore by a slice of the seven-layer chocolate, but for a real treat, it was all about cherry pie—a generous slice that was literally overflowing with cherries. And they weren't the large, canned kind of cherries either; they were small, tart little peas of sweetness that exploded with flavor. In the summer, a tall glass of milk was a necessity, but in the fall, coffee was the only way to go.

More often than not, it was standing room only in that old six-table shack. As is often the case for such local establishments, truck drivers had been the ones to really put the place on the map. They only had pie, and to get a long-haul truck driver to stop for that alone, Betty's had to be doing something right. And sometimes—just sometimes—it afforded other opportunities.

Vlad sat at the dinner counter inside the door of Betty's Pies, his plate nearly devoid of any evidence that a piece of cherry pie had ever lingered there. He sipped his cup of black coffee and cherished the warmth of it. More and more, he was finding it harder to get warm.

The young waitress wandered over and set the bill next to his plate. She had a hangdog look as her eyes darted between looking directly at Vlad's face and away again. Even with his stocking cap pulled down, she could see his scars. The young girl played with the rings that covered her fingers and clicked the piece of gum she'd been chewing for a long as Vlad had been there. She looked very kind and innocent.

Does she have any idea of what I am? he wondered, knowing she didn't.

"Can I get ya anything else, mister?" she asked.

"Nope. Just passing through and wanted to try a slice," Vlad said.

"Well?"

"Best cherry pie I've ever had."

She smiled and walked off with her pen tucked behind her ear.

The front door swung open with a *bang* as three men and a woman, all dressed in black, sauntered in with a communal look of ennui painted on their faces— not that there was much room for much of anything else on their faces between the piercings and makeup. Of the four, the girl might have used the least amount of foundation and eyeliner.

They wandered over to a side table and made a scene of the noise created by their arrival. They looked annoyed and irritated. The tallest of the four, the one who'd kicked the door open in the first place, sat with a *thud* and pulled out a cigarette and lighter. He made particular show of flicking the lighter open and taking a long, deep breath, twisting his head as he exhaled smoke in a cloud around them.

The waitress walked over diffidently and asked the lead goth to kindly put his cigarette out. "We don't allow smoking," she said, nodding toward the placard on the front door.

The young man, nineteen at the oldest, took a long

drag and made an even greater show of blowing the smoke directly at the waitress before he put it out on the table and ordered four black coffees for the table.

The waitress walked away quickly, coughing and looking frightened. She was near tears as she poured four cups of coffee from the large silver urn directly across from Vlad.

"Don't worry," he said, shaking his head at the silliness of it all. "They're just kids looking for attention. Don't let them get to you."

The waitress set down the cup she had been holding and turned to Vlad. "Maybe, but they don't have to be such dicks about it."

Vlad laughed loud enough that the table of self-absorbed goths turned their attention to him.

"Hey, mister," the waitress asked in a whisper, her eyes darting around his face, "can I ask you something?"

"You just did."

"That's not what I meant," she said, giggling.

Vlad smiled warmly. "Sure. Go ahead"

"What happened?" she asked, pointing at her own chin line.

Vlad reached up and touched his scars. "Hockey. Took a skate across the side of the face. Wasn't pretty."

The waitress made a hissing noise and clenched her teeth. "Jeez. I'm sorry. I didn't mean to pry."

"Meh, it's all right. I don't even notice it anymore."

Just then, one of the young men from the table yelled, "Hey Flo! How about those coffees?"

The rest of the table cackled at something they found funny about it all.

The waitress looked at them, then back at Vlad, releasing a frustrated little groan before she turned back to the coffee urn to finish pouring the coffee.

Vlad stared at the table from the corner of his eye, then pulled out his wallet and paid the bill in cash, leaving a generous tip. He stood and turned to leave, then looked out the window. Only his own car and the vehicle the rebellious youths had driven were parked in the lot. It had Iowa license plates.

After serving the coffees, the waitress fled into the kitchen. Vlad looked to see if she was out of sight before he walked over to the table casually, keeping his hands in the pockets of his hooded sweatshirt.

Four sets of eyeliner-circled eyes started up at him with contempt.

"What the fuck do you want?" the rude smoker asked.

Vlad looked over his shoulder to make sure the waitress was still in the kitchen before he removed his stocking cap and pulled back the neckline of his sweatshirt. The four sets of eyes grew larger when he asked, "Any of you been to the Witch Tree?"

CHAPTER 23

Police Chief Lockhart swiveled slightly from side to side on his diner counter stool. He had his earphones in and was enjoying pre-British-accent Madonna while he read over chat room transcripts. He and Deputy Lind hadn't gotten back into town until after three in the morning from their trip to Bemidji. He slept in beyond ten a.m. and was enjoying his first coffee of the day a little later than usual.

Freddie emerged from the kitchen, white towel in hand as he wiped away grease from slinging hash all morning. He wore a chef's jacket with his name on the breast pocket, though he opted for a blue bandana instead of the more formal toque. Freddie was respected as a chef by the surrounding populous as much, if not more, than any chef Lockhart had met in New York, Chicago, or L.A. He was just about as talented, too, from what Lockhart had tasted for himself.

Lockhart looked up and removed his ear buds. "Morning Freddie. Did you get any sleep?"

Freddie continued to rub his hands against the towel. He shrugged. "Couple hours I guess. I don't get too tired while I cook."

"Didn't know you were cooking today," Lockhart admitted with a clear tone of regret, "or I would've ordered more than bran flakes."

Lind smiled and tossed the towel over his shoulder. "No problem, Chief. Never a bad idea to stay regular."

Lockhart laughed heartily. Freddie wasn't known for his jokes, and Lockhart wasn't even sure if he'd meant it in jest, but sometimes the man just seemed to say exactly what was needed to lighten Lockhart's darkening mood. It was as much of a gift of the man's culinary prowess, and Lind didn't seem to do it on purpose. He just sort of had a knack for it.

"Watcha reading, Chief?" he asked.

Lockhart let the papers fall on the counter as he leaned back in his seat. He reached above his head and stretched high and wide. "Chat logs. These are the printouts from Scott's computer. I'm hoping to find something—anything that might point to where Scotty is."

Freddie stepped back and sat against the metal back service counter. "So you aren't buying that the kid just ran off?"

Lockhart gave him an incredulous glare in response.

"What about them two devil-worshipers you and Agent Rhodes interviewed in Grand Marais?"

Lockhart had considered it, of course, but he shook his head. "No probable cause. By Shadow's admission, both girls left the Witch Tree before Scott did. We need something more tangible if I'm gonna have the jurisdiction to question Shadow or Raven again. That Raven girl is holding something back for sure, but her overprotective mother is standing by her alibi, whether it's a bunch of bull or not."

Freddie grabbed a porcelain mug from the counter and poured himself a steaming cup of coffee. He didn't even bother to blow on it before taking a long, slurping sip. It was hot enough for Lockhart to easily smell the wafting aroma, but Freddie didn't seem to notice. He just licked his lips and looked grateful for the much-needed caffeine boost. "Raven, huh? Man, can't kids today just use real names? What about that Vlad guy? He must be in that log somewhere."

Lockhart grabbed the files again and flipped through the pages. "Tanya mentioned him a lot, like she has some kind of puppy-love crush on the creepy guy, but Scott never talked with Vlad directly. Also, we weren't able to get any hits on the alias in any of the databases."

"Ever thought of getting a warrant for *Tanya's* computer? She might be crazy enough to still be talking to the guy."

Lockhart drained the last of his own lukewarm coffee. "More jurisdiction issues, I'm afraid. Tanya's part of the FBI's ongoing investigation, and Bureau files are off limits to me these days."

Deputy Lind eyed Lockhart for a moment before gulping down the remainder of his still-steaming cuppa Joe. "And there's no way around that?"

"Maybe," Lockhart replied as he mulled the idea over, "but not right now. I have more pressing issues. For starters, I've gotta go tell Justin and Jess Erickson that their son is officially being considered a runaway. I don't know how they're gonna take that."

"Well, that's better than some of the alternatives, Chief," Freddie said, and Lockhart just nodded.

CHAPTER 24

Agent Caitlyn Rhodes had spent so much time following the Erickson lead that an important fact had escaped her: At least six other people were at the scene and were, as yet, unaccounted for.

In the time since Scott Erickson's missing persons report had come across the wire, there were over a dozen other missing persons reports from Minnesota, Wisconsin, and the Dakotas, and there was no immediate way to find out who might have come over from Canada. The border was even closer to the Witch Tree than Grand Marais.

Besides Shadow, Scott, and the still-unidentified Vlad, assuming that David Crowe was correct, there were still six unidentified people on the scene. Raven was a suspect, but her mother's alibi meant it was Tanya's word against theirs that the girl had been there.

Caitlyn was under pressure from her supervisor in the FBI to either clear the case or pass it off. The Ojibwe Nation had placed plenty of pressure on her and the Bureau to solve the crime that had taken place on their land, even if it meant she had to label the crime as something as simple as trespassing. Media relations had the tendency of ranking higher than justice under some circumstances.

Part of her wanted to call it a case of trespassing and write off the blood as an accident, but she couldn't get past the idea that information was being withheld, particularly in the case of that brat Raven.

Agent Rhodes's window for getting the case closed was rapidly shrinking, and she had to make progress quickly. In an effort to expedite the investigation, Caitlyn decided to concede that David Crowe's assessment of the crime scene might actually have been more accurate than she'd originally given him credit for. Not only that, but it also fit the profile. Scott, Raven, and Shadow were all seventeen or eighteen years old and white; at least Raven and Shadow came from middle- to upper-middleclass homes. Crowe had referred to the trespassers as "privileged," and while that was a relative term, it was likely that they would have seemed as such to Crowe.

Eight of the missing persons reports from the tri-state area involved teenagers. They were spread across three states, and there was no feasible way for Caitlyn to thoroughly investigate all the reports in a short amount of time, let alone get permission from her superiors to investigate kidnappings in conjunction with a blurred stain on some rocks on the shore of Lake Superior. There were still no DNA results, so Caitlyn couldn't even verify that the blood belonged to Scott Erickson in the first place, matching blood type aside. That made her give pause and wonder why Lockhart would have even agreed to go and investigate; there simply wasn't concrete evidence.

Agent Caitlyn Rhodes was exhausted. She hadn't slept well for several nights, and all the driving around with a former agent—an *exceedingly frustrating* former agent at that—had taken its toll. She needed coffee. Caitlyn decided to take the several-blocks walk to her favorite coffee shop in lieu of driving. The cold air offered a momentary shock and reprieve from her fatigue.

The ambiance of Cantabria Coffee Company was all at once inviting and numbing. Agent Rhodes felt so relaxed in the atmosphere of swirling coffee smells that she could have taken a nap and slept for days, all while sitting up in one of the chairs. Instead, she went for an iced espresso. She was mildly concerned that if she selected hot coffee, it would actually make her just want to curl up under a blanket and hibernate. The cool, syrupy jolt of icy-cold caffeine was just what she needed. She'd needed motivation, wherever she could find it. Her next course of action was important; she couldn't afford to waste any time, as a single bad lead could mean the end of the investigation.

It took until the end of her beverage to make her decision. She had to put her faith in David Crowe, and she needed to search for the other missing teens.

CHAPTER 25

All things considered, Police Chief Lockhart would have rather been sitting atop a stool at The Pit Stop with a beer and shot in front of him. Instead, he was perched behind his desk in the law enforcement office, reliving the conversation he'd just had. It was too early in the day for him to imbibe, but the Ericksons hadn't taken the news about their son well. He really couldn't blame them though. The only answers he'd given them were no answers at all. They were no closer to knowing where Scott was, and Lockhart had broken the news that officially, he would just be treated as a runaway. Scott would turn eighteen in less than a month, and it was impossible not to think he would never be seen again.

Lockhart leaned on his desk, his face cupped in his hands as he tried to gently massage the tension out of his temples. Even the tinkling of the bell that hung above the door to the law enforcement office chimed too loudly and grated against his back teeth.

"Chief?" Deputy Freddie Lind asked. "You okay?"

"Yeah Freddie. I'm fine," Lockhart lied without looking up.

"Are you ready to go?"

Lockhart grimaced to himself; he had totally forgotten. Freddie had recently informed him of a Crayton tradition regarding the recently deceased. Whereas some people visited graves on the anniversary of a death, the people of Crayton chose to visit on the first birthday after someone's passing. That particular day involved the celebration of what would have been the sixty-fifth birthday of Lockhart's predecessor, Chief John Donaldson. "Ready as I'll ever be Freddie,"

Lockhart said as he stood and grabbed his jacket from the coat rack next to the door. "Let's go."

Much like John Donaldson's well-attended funeral, the cemetery was filled with citizens there to pay their respects for the longtime police chief. Lockhart hadn't gotten much of a chance to get to know Donaldson during his track-down of The Taker, but he seemed like a good man, regardless of his choices in terms of fingerprinting most of town. The townspeople's demeanor reflected as much. Rows and rows of flowers lined the grave and adorned the tombstone. Some joked and reveled in stories, while others wept in near-silent reflection; the occasion was clearly meant to resemble more of a New Orleans-style wake than a solemn occasion, and as such, Lockhart realized just how large the shoes were that he was supposed to fill.

Freddie and Lockhart milled around for over an hour as people funneled in and out. Even though he felt guilty about it, Lockhart couldn't help but feel a little bored. His eyes wandered around the surprisingly large graveyard. Some markers were over 100 years old. Others were so worn and weather beaten that they were almost unreadable. Only close inspection would show that there had ever been any etching in the stone. Some didn't appear to have ever been etched; just blank markers for unnamed bodies.

Lockhart probably wouldn't have noticed the blank headstones if not for the fact that Deputy Lind looked to take special care as he walked around them. Lockhart's first instinct was that the graves were empty or simply reserved plots. "Hey Freddie," he had to ask as they walked out of the cemetery, "what's with the blank stones?"

Freddie looked over his shoulder and paused.

"Unmarked graves," he whispered, as if the ones lying beneath might hear him and be insulted.

"There are over twenty of them. What happened?"

Freddie raised an eyebrow. "Ya mean you don't know why the kids always spray paint the city limits sign to say 'CRAZYTOWN'?"

Actually, Lockhart did know. In one of their rare talks, Chief Donaldson had explained the strange attacks and disappearances that had happened in Crayton during the late 1920s and '30s. Lind nodded his head backward toward the gravestones.

Lind explained, "Chief, those blank tombstones are markers for people who were never identified, but the town just couldn't let them go unburied. That was around the time when people did their best to celebrate people's lives instead of reminding themselves of how many people were dying."

"Wow. That's depressing." Lockhart saw Freddie's face drop, but he didn't say anything more.

At that moment, Lockhart saw a shape in the corner of his eye, like someone standing there staring at him and it wasn't the first time that day he had noticed it. By the time he turned, he realized no one was there.

"Hey Freddie, you ever get the feeling like you're being watched?"

"No," Freddie said bluntly.

"Oh, okay. What's on the docket today, Deputy?"

Freddie shook his head as his dress shoes click-clacked along the downtown sidewalk. He pulled a pack of cigarettes from his breast pocket and lit one. He took a long, contemplative drag before giving his answer with a cloud of smoke. "I think we need to take the truck back to the Ericksons. It is theirs, after all—and the last thing their boy touched, for all they know.

Might give 'em a little peace of mind."

"I doubt that," Lockhart said, "but I suppose we should give it back to its rightful owners anyway."

CHAPTER 26

There was no shortage of work for Agent Caitlyn Rhodes over the following two days. As Tanya Murphy had admitted to trespassing on Native American land, Caitlyn was well within her jurisdiction to take Tanya's computer into evidence, not to mention book and arrest her on federal charges. She heard from the local police that Tanya had put up no end of argument when they'd showed up to seize her electronics; confidentially, they wanted to just zap her with a tazer. Personally, Caitlyn would have been more inclined to subdue her friend Raven, but she still couldn't find an angle to disprove the girl's alibi, provided so conveniently by her mother. Agent Rhodes had to rely on her computer techs for that.

Within a 200-mile radius of the Witch Tree, without crossing the Canadian Border, five teenage boys and two teenage girls had been reported missing in the last week. While Caitlyn wasn't able to easily obtain records from Canada, she was willing to dismiss the possibilities of those kids disappearing due to their having to cross the border. Security had grown ever tighter over the last decade, thanks to international unease, and even the most rebellious kids weren't likely to go through so much red tape. If their teenage angst had carried them to such extremes, there wasn't much Caitlyn could do—at least not in terms of investigating.

All seven of the reported missing teens were Caucasian. Of those, the closest to the Bemidji field office turned out to be a bust; it only took a phone call to blow the suspicions out of the water. The boy's mother believed her ex-husband had absconded with the teen, and she was sure he would call sooner or later. When asked why she filled out the missing persons report, the woman said, "Because I want that stupid S.O.B. of an ex-husband to sweat it out in jail." Besides that, the boy had no links to the occult or Satanism. According to his mother, he was "too lazy for anything like that—just like his good-for-nothing-father."

The next closest was just outside of Duluth. As Duluth was where the computer techs would be running the diagnostics on Tanya's computer, Caitlyn would finally get a chance to fall asleep in her own bed.

Agent Rhodes had spent a large part of her life in Minnesota, most of that in Duluth. It was her town. She knew the best routes to avoid icy, hilly drives in the winter. She knew where to get a double Maker's Mark that didn't cost twice as much as a single shot. She knew the best place for breakfast at any time of the day.

Even in what Duluth referred to as 'traffic,' Caitlyn could get anywhere in less than twenty minutes. In the summer, tourists flooded the city on their way up the North Shore. In the autumn, people came just to see the changing seasons. In the winter, endless teams of youth hockey players crammed the ice arenas.

Life was easier there, at least for Caitlyn Rhodes. Sometimes—just sometimes—life got a whole lot more complicated. One minute she might be working a case involving illegal wire transfers, the next she might find herself on a rock cliff just south of the Canadian border in an attempt to solve a missing persons case.

Sometimes, there were missing persons cases that involved people like Brandon Gillespie, age seventeen, reported missing by his distraught mother and father just one day after the blood was found at the Witch

Tree. Strangely, the living room of the Gillespie house looked much the same as those of Raven and Shadow: a simple, middleclass home, with family pictures on the tables, a crucifix on the wall and floral patterns on several pieces of furniture. It was all very quiet and reserved...all except for Brandon's room.

Caitlyn wasn't able to work off of the strongest profile for her investigation, but it definitely appeared that Brandon fit the bill. Darkness was definitely the motif: black walls, black candles, and posters with pentagrams and skulls. Scattered around the room were CDs by bands like The Damned, The Cure, and The Cult, not to mention more than a few bands that Rhodes had never heard of.

The Gillespies had last seen their son the morning before the supposed ritual had taken place at the Witch Tree. He had left for school in the morning, and he didn't return that night. According to the parents, it wasn't uncommon for Brandon to go unseen in the evenings, since both of them had full-time jobs and often worked late. Loner that he was, the boy tended to spend his evenings in his room. Most mornings, he'd sneak out of the house on his way to school and avoid them altogether. It wasn't until the school called Mrs. Gillespie to inquire about Brandon's absence from school that they knew something was wrong. When they didn't see him the next day, they filed the police report.

Caitlyn convinced the parents to let them take Brandon's computer for analysis. Between Shadow and Brandon, the tech guys were going to be busy.

For the most part, Agent Caitlyn Rhodes had a professional, if not solid relationship with the men and women who worked the Duluth FBI Cyber Crimes

Division. Really, there was only one man in the division whom Caitlyn avoided talking to, so she was annoyed at the irony that he, of all people, was put in charge of looking into Tanya's computer.

Nick Allen, in his short-sleeved dress shirt and tie, swiveled slightly in his cubicle office chair. His attention was focused on dual computer screens, and he typed rapidly while bobbing his head to music blaring out of his headphones. He took the occasional loud slurp from a can of Mountain Dew and didn't notice Agent Rhodes standing beside him. Perhaps more annoying that his lackluster communication skills and almost childlike physical behavior was that Nick Allen was just about the best person in the department at his job.

When people came to his cube, Nick had the strange habit of turning in his chair slowly around, like a James Bond villain. He sat up completely erect, as if his identity required a remarkable reveal, like someone made over on a reality show. Sometimes, he even pretended like he was petting an invisible cat.

Caitlyn knocked on the top of the cube wall. Right on cue, and much to her dismay, Nick did his dramatic turn as he let out a long, snakelike, "Yeeesss…?"

Caitlyn kept her composure and resisted walking away to find someone else to work on the case. She reminded herself that as awful as putting up with him was, it was for the greater good. "Agent Rhodes. I'm here about the results from Tanya's computer. Were you able to recover anything off her Internet history?"

Allen's eyebrow raised in a suggestive arch that looked more comical than serious, especially when accentuated by his horn-rimmed glasses and mild case of adult acne, probably caused by the copious amounts of fats and sugars he always seemed to shovel in his mouth. It was a wonder he stayed so skinny. "Well," Allen said in a sarcastic tone, "she *did* delete her Internet history." He let out a forced laugh and slurped another mouthful of yellowish-green carbonated go-juice.

Caitlyn didn't follow. "So does that mean we can't get anything off of the computer?"

Allen let out a condescending snort. "Not hardly. Nothing is ever really deleted off a computer. You can find anything if you know what you're doing—which *I* do." Nick Allen spun back to face his computer monitors and typed away at an impressive speed.

Caitlyn set her hand on the cube wall to steady herself as she leaned over the desk. "You can retrieve a *deleted* Internet history?" she asked in disbelief.

Nick Allen's typing stopped for a moment, and his head turned slightly, just enough so Caitlyn could see his eyes bulging from the sides of their sockets while he tried to look down her blouse. "Sure, as long as you have the right...*tool,*" he said with all the grace of a horny fourteen-year-old boy.

Caitlyn wasn't afraid to confront such sad attempts. She moved just inches away from Nick Allen's face and looked him up and down. "Mr. Allen, your double-entendre is as weak as your upper body."

Nick Allen leapt back in shock. "Hey! I do forty push-ups every night before bed."

Caitlyn held her stare. "So do I...in a row and on my toes."

Nick Allen's mouth fell open just slightly. "Whoa! That's hot," he said.

A smile crept across Caitlyn's face; she had to give him credit for trying. "What did you find on the computer?"

Nick Allen gawked for a few moments longer before he turned back to his computer. "Uh...anything and everything. What is it you're looking for?"

Caitlyn smiled a look of triumph. She knew Nick Allen would no doubt mistake it for flirting, but she couldn't help it. She was finally making some headway. "Let's start with her Internet history and any chat logs that might be connected with sites she's visited in the last week."

Nick Allen hit Ctrl+P on his keyboard, and the printer next to his cube whirred to life.

CHAPTER 27

Crayton Chief of Police Darren Lockhart sat alone in the living room of the bed-and-breakfast that he called home. Only the occasional tap of his footF and the *tick-tock* of the wall clock interrupted the silence. From time to time, his view would focus on another part of the room, with no particular interest. Even the idea of getting up to make himself a sandwich for lunch came with some level of disinterest that immediately pushed it from his mind.

Through it all, he was distracted enough that the sound of Jess Erickson's voice gave him a start. "Hello, Chief," she said meekly from the foyer doorway that separated the entryway from the living room of the cozy place.

"Jess," Lockhart said, standing politely to greet a lady. "I'm sorry. I didn't hear you come in." Lockhart wasn't even sure if she'd bothered to knock or not.

To this, the distraught mother said nothing. She moved toward one of the empty easy chairs, and her ethereal gait made it look like she'd just walked through walls to get where she was going.

Lockhart waited for her to sit before he sat himself. "How are you doing, Jess?"

Mrs. Erickson made no immediate response. Her eyes, as they had been since Lockhart first delivered the news, were focused on the ground. It wasn't until that moment that Lockhart realized she was carrying a laptop with her, but he didn't say a thing about it.

"You know," Jess said finally, as if telling a story to the floor, "the doctors said Justin and I wouldn't be able to have kids. They said our biology was incompatible or something like that. They had a fancier way of saying it, of course, but I think that was just to make themselves feel better about us failing to make a baby."

Lockhart settled back in his chair, content to let Jess speak more words than he had ever heard from her.

"When Scotty finally did come along, we knew he was a miracle. It didn't matter what the doctors said. It was God's will that Scotty came into our lives." Jess pulled the laptop up to her chest and hugged it tightly with both arms. "He was a miracle and a blessing, but that didn't make things easy. He got sick a few times—really bad sick, and we had to pray over him a lot. Once he got the flu, and I really thought we were going to lose our little boy." Jess looked up at Lockhart, her eyes probing him. "I hope you don't think me a fool, Chief. People from big cities and those without faith tend judge when somebody says they're praying for their sick child. They put their faith in medicine and technology to pull them through, but my husband and I believe in Jesus Christ, the great physician. We always have. Even in the hardest times, we've kept our faith that there is a Higher Power looking out for good people."

Lockhart interlocked his fingers and smiled at her, nodding to prod her to go on.

Jess gently set the laptop down on the table next to the chair. She slid so slightly forward in her chair that Lockhart barely noticed she was leaning in, barely even in a seated position any longer. "Chief Lockhart, I know you're the new lawman around here, but my husband and I are good people. No matter what anybody thinks of the clothes he wears or the music he listens to, our son Scotty is a good boy who just...lost his way. That don't mean we ever stopped loving him. We never will."

Lockhart was at a loss for words and only managed

to stutter, "Mrs. Erickson, I—" before she waved him off.

"He is still out there, Chief Lockhart. I don't believe he wants to be where he is. I also don't care that he's almost grown in the government's eyes. Scotty's a little boy lost, and he needs someone to keep looking for him."

Lockhart sat in abject silence. The woman, not all that much older than he was, had succeeded at making his heart feel even heavier at the realization of his own wretched impotence.

As she stood up to leave, Jess tapped the top of the laptop. "This is Scotty's. He paid for it himself with money he earned mowing lawns and doing odd jobs around town. Like I said, Chief, he's a good boy. A boy like that doesn't just run away." With that, she walked to the front door, then turned one last time. "It's still logged into his e-mail and Facebook accounts. I hope that will help."

Lockhart sat on the patio swing of the bed-and-breakfast and gently pushed himself back and forth in the sunny, but cold October afternoon. His attention was focused on reading the printout of Scott Erickson's user history from DarkBeliever.com, a website devoted to the occult, Satanism, and aggressively anti-Christian beliefs; the boy had it set to his homepage, which was interesting in its own right. Lockhart has been so used to having other investigators with him, that he hadn't bothered to do more than check the computer's search history when the family first made the report. It was a mistake he vowed he would atone for.

The site itself was nothing Lockhart hadn't seen before. *Everyone wants to believe in something, even if that something is nothing*, he reminded himself. Lockhart was far more interested in the forum history shared between Tanya "$h@d0w" Murphy and Scott "dr@k3" Erickson.

A good portion of the forum entitled "Beyond Natural" involved users posting links and pictures to places around the world that were supposedly haunted or were confirmed locations of Satanic possession. The Winchester House, Eastern State Penitentiary, Bell Hall, and Bhangarh were all listed. Farther down the list, user dr@k3 posted a link about "The D3v1l's K3ttl3" (The Devil's Kettle), a location not far from Grand Marais. Shadow had countered with "Th3 W!+ch +r33" with the added comment, "as recommended by Vl@d."

It was a simple, but surprisingly effective method for Scotty and Raven to cover their tracks. Subject locations like Eastern State or Winchester House could yield search results in the hundreds or thousands due to their storied and checkered histories. The Witch Tree and The Devil's Kettle were smaller, regional, and lesser known. Just by replacing letters with symbols and numbers, Googlers could render a standard Internet search all but useless without knowing what to look for and where.

Unfortunately, it didn't look as though the man called Vl@d had any direct contact with Tanya or Scott through the forum, and all the info from him was secondhand through Tanya/$h@d0w. He hadn't left any postings on the site, at least under the usernames Vlad, Vl@d, V1@d, or any other combination that Lockhart could come up with.

The site didn't post details in regard to the supposed haunted locations or what was supposed to have gone on there. There was also no mention of what

Scott and Tanya had planned to do there. However, Scott had stayed logged into his Facebook account and hadn't logged out before he disappeared. When the computer was checked, the social networking site was still up and running. There were several back-and-forth messages between Scott and Tanya. Of course, Lockhart needed the assistance of Deputy Lind to figure the site out, but the information was right there—all of it. In all, there were months' worth of correspondences, including where, when, and what. It all sounded harmless, but more importantly, more than a few messages were about The Witch Tree.

According to the messages, Scott had made no mention of wanting to run away or not returning home, and neither did Tanya. There were no posts or even veiled promises/threats that he was thinking of doing anything extreme. Tanya had told him what was to happen, an agenda created by the almighty Vlad, and Scott had agreed without hesitation. The timestamp between her message, telling him about doing a ritual at the Witch Tree and his response wasn't even a minute apart.

None of it came across as the kind of talk a kid fed up with his parents and seeking emancipation would say. He sounded more like a love-struck kid who would have done anything the object of his affection, Tanya, wanted:

> **Shadow: r u in 4 2nite?**
> **Drake: yes**
> **Shadow: do u remember where 2 meet?**
> **Drake: yes**
> **Shadow: u arent goin to chcken out r u?**
> **Drake: no, i can't wait**
> **Shadow: u better be. vlad will be pissed if we bale**

Drake: i'm with you all the way…NEthing U want

By the time Lockhart had finished reading all the messages and forum posts, he was positive—returned truck or not—that Scott Erickson had not run away from home. The truth was, the boy may not have even left The Witch Tree…alive.

Lockhart lowered his head, his eyes shifting away from the text in his hands. He couldn't stop thinking about Scott. He could still see the look on Jess Erickson's face: the lines in the corners of her mouth from where it turned down in melancholy; the anguish in her eyes every time Lockhart showed up at her door without her son in tow.

Taking back the truck had been hard enough, as it was just another reminder for the Ericksons that their son was gone. *That old Chevy truck, the one with the shiny new trailer hitch.*

Lockhart stood abruptly, nearly smashing his head on the crossbar above the rocker. His head was spinning; he had a call to make.

CHAPTER 28

The choir of wailing screams was a cacophony of pain and frustration. The sound itself was to be expected and even passé, but Vlad found the reaction a bit ironic. He tended to think kids who spoke about pain, darkness, and the devil were a different breed. Piercings, tattoos, burns, scars from cutting, and whatever it might be, pain was somehow wired differently in their minds. If nothing else, they should have been a bit more familiar with the reality that life isn't fair.

Then again, things always seemed worse when it came to being locked in a cage or chained to a wall. An injection of Stadol or Demerol might have made things a bit more bearable. Of course drugs would be accompanied by side effects, and he was ill-equipped to handle respiratory or cardiac complications in relation to medication.

Of course, it was all a bit like splitting hairs, considering what he might do to any number of them, but there was no need to put them through any more pain than necessary. He wasn't a sadist after all. In truth, Vlad considered himself to be somewhere between a pioneer and a masochist. Then again, the line between the two often seemed skewed.

His feet clanged up the turn-of-the-century metal mesh stairway to the upper levels of the building. It was the kind of rusty *clank* that gave off the sound of things that no longer existed in the living world. Past the long-ago-used machinery and broken-out office windows, the silence in that corner of Vlad's home was broken only by a weak threat. It was the cross to bear that saddled any man willing to do what others weren't.

One black-clad teenager in particular seemed to have great conflicts with being chained; of course it was the rude one who'd insisted on ashing his cigarette on the table at Betty's Pies back in Two Harbors. It was really no wonder that he, of all of them, would be the one to insist on constant attention.

Vlad walked up to him gently, as if he were approaching an injured stray dog, and inspected the leather restraints that held the boy's waist and torso against the wall. They had a faux fur lining and didn't seem to be aggravating the boy's skin. The chain that hung around his neck was attached to the wall as well, but it was at least an inch away from choking him. The second leather strap, the one securing his forehead, showed the most strain; his skin was tight as he pulled and struggled against that particular restraint. "You should stop struggling. You're just going to hurt yourself unnecessarily," Vlad said patiently, as if he were speaking to a small child throwing a temper tantrum.

The youth responded with a long string of uncouth and largely nonsensical cursing.

Vlad leaned in closer. Despite the boy's attempts to darken the surrounding skin with makeup, his eyes were actually quite beautiful: a soft, blue-gray reminiscent of those on a husky dog.

It was there, standing only inches from the boy's face, that Vlad suddenly saw a flash of white light. He staggered backward and, above the ringing in his ears, heard the sound of a loud choking gurgle emanating from the wall. When his eyes focused and he regained his vision, Vlad saw that the boy's forehead strap had come loose from all the struggling, and the young man's head had crashed into Vlad's brow with a wickedly painful and violent head-butt. The warm trickle of blood traced its way down Vlad's face, enough to coat a good portion of the back of his hand when he wiped it from his eyes. The laceration was deep enough that when Vlad ran his fingers across his brow, he could immediately tell it would require several stitches.

The momentum unleashed by the strap breaking made the boy's head drive forward so far that he nearly strangled himself with the chain around his neck. He hung there, gasping and coughing for breath.

Vlad lost his composure and grabbed the boy's wrist. He forced it back hard and felt the snap and grind of bone reverberating through his own hand. Vlad offered no apology as the boy bellowed in pain; he knew it was only the start of misery for his stubborn and writhing captive. He grabbed the boy by his hair and slammed his head back against the steel wall plate. The young man let out a groan, and his gray eyes rolled in their sockets. Vlad clenched his jaw and leaned in. "I'd say this is going to hurt me more than it will you, but the fact is, it's going to hurt us both—a lot."

CHAPTER 29

Agent Caitlyn Rhodes sat on the patio dining area of a small soup-and-sandwich shop off Superior Street in Duluth. From that vantage point, she could watch both the occasional foot traffic of tourists and the lake behind the Fitger's Brewery complex.

It had been easy for the FBI computer department to pull up Tanya's Internet history; however, actually tracking down Vlad was a different matter. Wherever Vlad had sent his e-mails from, he had access to advanced computer equipment and the know-how to utilize multiple servers. Nick Allen was fairly certain that they'd be able to find him eventually, though it would take time—something Caitlyn didn't seem to have enough of, no matter how thin she tried to spread herself.

She was at a dead end and frustrated. The computer history didn't yield anything of much use. There were long, rambling e-mails back and forth between Tanya and Vlad, mostly a jumble of dark images and horrible poetry. Whoever Vlad was, he was a smooth talker. He knew how to say all the right things to a girl like Tanya, and the way she responded to him made it clear that she was easily manipulated by the cyber-Casanova.

Agent Rhodes put out a search for the 'Vlad' in the Bureau's sexual offenders database, to no avail. She knew it was frivolous anyway, since most sexual predators don't use such a high degree of cautiousness. There tends to be a brazenness in acts of sexual assault and violence. Internet predators might take their time to feel out their bait, but there was always that moment when it went to the next level: naked pictures, propositions, and explicit sexual conversations, all of which lead to the inevitable request to meet. Vlad had done none of that. He just sweet-talked the girl, and there wasn't even a hint that he wanted to exchange pictures, nor was there any e-mail containing an actual meeting proposal. If he had suggested they meet, it had to have been on an Internet forum or via instant messaging. There was nothing in her e-mail or social networking accounts to indicate that he'd manipulated her into a face-to-face, and besides that, Agent Rhodes knew he didn't ultimately meet her alone. At least Scott was there, if not a half-dozen other people. In any case, Vlad did not act like a typical sexual predator.

Besides that, Caitlyn had the feeling that the case was about more than just Tanya or Scott Erickson.

Agent Rhodes sat alone on the patio. Winter was on its way, and the air was chilly, with a northern charge to it. She had lived in Duluth long enough to feel in the air that it would snow soon. Caitlyn loved eating out in the open air, though, and took every opportunity to do so—especially in the cold weather, when she could indulge in her favorite temptation, beer cheese soup. Another perk of living on the Wisconsin border was the ready availability of the byproduct of too much beer, cheese, and time on someone's hands. Add a turkey club, and it didn't get any better for her. Caitlyn needed the comfort; the investigation was slipping through her fingers, and her leads were next to nothing.

Caitlyn had hoped for more from Brandon's computer, but the disk was encrypted and was far more difficult to glean information from. Nick Allen made sure to point out that it was not impossible for a genius like himself, but it would be difficult and time-consuming nonetheless. Caitlyn opted to focus her resources on tracking Vlad down. She needed something big—and fast.

Her soup cooled as quickly as she could eat it. The wind blew off the lake in small bursts, as if just to remind Caitlyn that weather in Duluth was its own entity. The cry of seagulls split the air as they floated above her, always flying against the wind and begging for scraps. Unlike the tourists in Canal Park, Caitlyn wasn't so easily swayed.

She finished her meal and carried her dishes inside to spare the inappropriately dressed server the need to walk back into the cold air. For all the time Caitlyn spend delving into the psychology of criminals, there were some things she just couldn't figure out. One of them was why anyone would wear a t-shirt in forty-degree weather, on the cusp of Minnesota winter. She decided he must have been an unwitting college kid from out of town.

Before leaving, Caitlyn pulled out a folded piece of paper that contained the artist's rendering of Tanya's description of Vlad. She showed it to her server. "Have you seen this man?" she asked.

The inappropriately clothed server took the piece of paper and looked at it for just a moment before shaking his head. "Nope. Sorry. Doesn't look familiar."

Caitlyn wasn't surprised; it was a vague description at best. By Tanya's own admission, it was dark, and she'd only seen Vlad's face for moments at a time, when the lightning flashed and the candles flickered. Still, the picture had been sent out on the wire to local police departments and the state highway patrol, just in case.

Agent Rhodes checked her watch. She had twenty minutes until she had to be back at the office for a requested status update on the investigation into the desecration of Ojibwe land. Of course she'd hoped for more information going into the meeting. Ideally, she would have preferred to have a link between Tanya, Raven, Brandon, and Vlad, but until the computer team could access the secrets lurking in Brandon's hard drive, all she had to go on was Tanya's admission that she and Scott Erickson were at the Witch Tree with several others for some kind of Vlad-officiated Satanic ritual. Raven had been given an alibi by her mother, and Scott was effectively determined a runaway following the recovery of the Ericksons' truck. Caitlyn needed more information, and she simply didn't have it.

Back at the FBI Duluth Resident Agency offices, the only forthcoming information was in the form of her perceived status report. The assistant director of Criminal, Cyber, Response, and Service Branch, Sondra Chatman, didn't need to be in the room; the dictum laid on Rhodes via teleconference was more than enough.

"Agent Rhodes, you do understand that our country has had something of a checkered history with the Native American people, correct?" Director Chatman's tone was without pretense, as would be expected from one of the FBI's pioneer female agents.

"Yes, ma'am," Rhodes replied respectfully.

"And you are aware that with media and social networking being what they are, scrutiny is at a level the Bureau has never seen before, are you not?"

"Yes, ma'am," Rhodes repeated, her hands starting to sweat.

"And you are aware that the allocation of federal agents is a very important responsibility, correct?"

"I am, ma'am."

Director Chatman paused, her eyes staring into a laptop webcam, but somehow still able to pierce through Agent Rhodes—or maybe even a bulletproof vest. "Then I must admit I am somewhat flummoxed to discern exactly what in the hell you've been doing for the last three days. Your responsibility was to go up to Grand Portage, take a statement, and close the case as quickly as possible, so as to maintain healthy relations with the Ojibwe Nation."

Rhodes didn't respond this time. She wasn't sure what she could say at that moment to explain herself. She also wasn't sure if Chatman had any desire to hear her speak.

"Do you have an explanation for me, Agent Rhodes? Can you tell me why you associated yourself with a former agent-turned-keystone cop, took him out of his jurisdiction, and made him privy to a federal investigation?"

Rhodes hesitated until she was sure Director Chatman was actually waiting for an answer. "Well, ma'am, Chief Lockhart had filed a missing persons report and—"

"Agent Rhodes, I'm not interested in the poor rationalization you've created in your own mind to justify this misallocation of resources as a noble cause, or a legal one for that matter. I'm giving you three days to close up this investigation, which you've somehow managed to turn into a goat rodeo."

Rhodes almost laughed at the metaphor, but she knew better.

"And Agent—mind you, I use that title loosely—the results of your investigation will absolutely reflect upon your future service in this agency. You've made your bed. I sure hope it's comfortable."

The screen switched off, and Rhodes balled up her fists in frustration. She hadn't been talked down that badly since she was a child. Then again, to be fair, she had acted nearly so impulsively in just about the same amount of time. Director Chatman had been right about everything. Rhodes's actions had been careless and stupid, and that had muddied the entire investigation.

To make matters worse, Lockhart hadn't actually helped anything. Thankfully, that was something she wouldn't have to worry about. She only hoped her own fate didn't match his.

CHAPTER 30

"You know this doesn't exactly fall within the Bureau's definition of 'legal,' right, *Mr*. Lockhart?"

Lockhart had to laugh at the FBI forensic specialist's emphasis on the commonplace title. He'd pulled some strings to forgo the chain of command and get a new forensic evaluation of the Ericksons' truck.

"We already checked the truck for prints. What a pain in the ass. This is one big truck." The specialist patted the side of the truck bed with his latex-gloved hand.

"I know," Lockhart said. "I was there when you did it the first time, so I know you didn't check where I want you to check now."

"And where would that be?"

As a boy, Lockhart's father—after retiring from the Navy—had made a living moving and towing sailboats. It was a niche job, but it paid well. Rich people could rarely be bothered to move their own boats, so they hired people to sail them from port to port and, on some odd occasions, even tow them over dry land.

When his father was actually home, he and Lockhart spent most of their together time aboard those boats, usually on fishing trips. Darren often helped his father hook the boats up to trailer hitches and tow them to and from whatever lake his father had chosen for that particular vacation.

So, it was not unknown to Lockhart that not all trailer hitches line up perfectly with the boat trailer. Some would need a little pull or lift to get the adjustment just right, and sometimes a person needed to brace themselves.

"We already dusted the bumper and the hitch."

"And?"

"Nothin'."

"What about underneath?" Lockhart asked.

The specialist gave a cockeyed stare as Lockhart hooked his hand under the bumper, as if he were trying to pull the truck backward. "Why didn't you just print it yourself?"

Lockhart smiled smoothly. "Why screw up a paint-by-numbers job when Van Gogh can do the real thing?"

The specialist shook his head at the ham-handed compliment and set to work. Within minutes, a "son-of-a…" emanated from underneath the rear axle of the Ericksons' truck. The specialist pulled himself back to his feet with a clear set of four fingerprint samples and frowned. "I can't believe I missed these."

"You didn't," Lockhart assured him. "On further rumination, on a hunch, you took it upon yourself to seek permission from local law enforcement to recheck the truck for more evidence not originally requested by the agent in charge of the investigation—a check that turned up evidence that could solve a possible kidnapping."

The specialist looked up from the samples, surprised at Lockhart's summary of events, and gave a slow, appreciative nod for the credit Lockhart was giving him.

Then again, credit and kudos were the last thing Lockhart was concerned with. Lockhart's theory was that whoever had taken Scotty, be it the Vlad character or someone else, needed to cover his tracks. Something had clearly gone wrong, and the kidnapper needed to get the truck off the grid. He could have ditched it, but he was smart. Returning the truck changed how investigations would proceed, even if they would proceed at all. So, he towed another vehicle with him when he brought the truck back. He pulled the truck just far enough off the road so he wouldn't leave any extra tracks, wiped down the bumper where he thought he touched it, then unhitched the other vehicle from the trailer and drove off in it. It was insanely complicated, but brilliant at the same time—the way criminal minds often worked. Lockhart himself would have never thought of it had it not been for the presence of the hitch scuffs, and it certainly wouldn't have stuck without the matching prints. Whoever had done it was willing to commit to their crime in ways that Lockhart had rarely seen, even in twenty years with the Bureau. He seemed to be dealing with a mastermind, of sorts—and one with a nasty evil streak. "Can you tell if they're the same as the prints you pulled from the cab of the truck?" Lockhart asked.

The specialist shook his head. "Those were left-handed. The position of these suggests they are from the right hand, but they do appear to be from the same person, from what I can recall."

"Wait, the prints in the cab were all from a left hand? Even the ones on the gear shift?"

"Yeah," the specialist said, otherwise preoccupied inspecting the prints in his hand.

Why would someone use their left hand to shift a truck in gear if the shift is on the right side of a steering wheel? Lockhart rubbed his chin.

The specialist looked the Crayton chief of police in the eyes and grinned slightly. "I suppose I should still run them against the FBI database. It's proper procedure when a forensic tech uncovers evidence."

Nothing ever really changes, Lockhart mused. When he'd been with the Bureau, things still worked the same. All anyone really wanted was to look like a case-breaker, a hero, of sorts. If finding Scotty Erickson meant giving the credit to some forensics specialist whose name he didn't even know, that was fine with him. He'd gladly take the relieved look on the faces of the boy's parents as his only accolades.

The specialist packed up his kit. "I suppose you'd like to be kept in the loop, right, Chief?"

Lockhart answered with a pleased smile.

Beads of perspiration ran down to the small of Darren Lockhart's back, leaving an icy trail in their wake, the first sign that he was about to break into a heavy sweat.

The temperature was only fifty degrees, and he was nearly a mile into his run before he had a good sweat going. In any case, it felt good to just get out on the road without having to think about anything besides where each foot was going to land.

Chief Lockhart had never been the kind of man who could easily turn his mind off. Twenty years of criminal investigation had changed him from a man who could kick back with a beer and leave work at work to a man who saw crime everywhere and always worked out ways to see inside of it and understand it.

At one time, it had been murderers and thieves; now it was kids trying to get drunk or high and adults who...well, were also trying to get drunk or high. Small-town life was a bit simpler—as was the urge to get away.

Murray Head crooned about "One Night in Bangkok" as Lockhart plodded along. He told himself he ran to stay in shape. At forty-two, it was getting harder and harder to keep the weight off. The truth was, he ran for the same reasons that he trained jiu-jitsu in Bemidji: It was a way to escape.

Lockhart ran from the Ericksons and their pain that he knew might never go away. He ran from Agent Rhodes, who reminded him of all the things he no longer was. He ran from Crayton, a place that needed a chief of police about as much as a cactus needed watering.

He ran until all he could think about was the burning urgency for air in his lungs, the pounding pain in his knees, the sweat that ran down his forehead to burn his eyes.

Then he ran back home—home to the bed-and-breakfast where he rested his head, even if his mind seldom ever dozed off.

While he was out, two new boarders had arrived in town: Skip and Nancy from the east metro. The moment Lockhart walked through the B-and-B front door, Joy introduced him formally as "our chief of police." Lockhart felt embarrassed to stand in front of them, stinking of sweat and representing the city law enforcement. Both new boarders exhibited the brief look of confusion that people got when they learned that the town's chief lawman made his home in a bed-and-breakfast.

Lockhart did his best to keep the mood light. "It's just easier to live here, with all the trouble Jill and Joy make."

The sisters blushed, and all shared a polite, albeit forced laugh. Lockhart excused himself upstairs to take a shower, and Jill called to let him know that dinner would be ready in half an hour.

Lockhart took his time. First, he let the cold water

hit his skin and suck the air from his chest. His muscles clenched as he acclimated to the temperature and his body cooled itself from the sweat. Gradually he turned up the heat and let the hot, steaming water wash over him. His neck and upper back were knotted from tension and the effects of aging. Grappling and running kept him active and strong, but his physical strength rarely kept up with his will; it seemed he woke with new pains every day. Lockhart stood there in the small bathtub and let the showerhead cascade the cleansing water across his shoulders. He had to stoop to fit his six-four frame under the spray.

As he closed his eyes, he saw Scott Erickson there in the darkness. He saw Scott's body on the cliff edge and a halo of blood expanding out from the boy's head. Seven figures dressed completely in black stood around the Witch Tree and stared at the lifeless body sprawled before them. A central figure looked large against a sky of swirling clouds.

It was a horrible image, and only the warm caress of the water kept Lockhart grounded from the parts of his mind that pulled him into the darkness of the world he'd lived for all too long. Slowly, he started to feel the warmth drain back out of the water, and he quickly washed his hair before facing another icy shock.

Lockhart wiped the steam off the bathroom mirror. For just a moment before the glass started to fog up again, a face stared back at him—one he thought he recognized. It was the face of a highly devoted, trained, decorated federal agent, but the swirling steam clouded the image until it all but disappeared.

A t-shirt and jeans replaced a blue police uniform as Lockhart transitioned to Crayton evening wear. He met Joy, Jill, Skip, and Nancy downstairs for a dinner of broiled walleye and steamed vegetables.

Without a doubt, Deputy Lind was the best chef in the area, but when it came to home cooking and the requisite feeling of nostalgia that seemed to present itself with each meal, Jill and Joy were second only to a person's own mother.

As usual, the meal was fairly quiet, occasional bits of small talk breaking up the sounds of clanging flatware and chewing, followed by a chorus of "Mmm…" praises for the delectable meal. Skip and Nancy were from the Twin Cities, heading up north for a late-season vacation. They had decided at the last minute to stop in Crayton and admitted that until they'd driven through—quite by accident since their GPS didn't even register the place—they'd never heard of the town.

After dinner, as Joy was in the kitchen preparing dessert and Jill toed the invasion-of-privacy line with her boarders via a plethora of questions about their lives and family, Deputy Lind made a rare appearance at the bed-and-breakfast. A gentle knock at the front door preceded Lind's near-silent entry into the front foyer.

"Hi Freddie," Jill said excitedly. "We don't see you much around here."

"Evening, Jill," Freddie said, politely taking off his policeman's cap. "I came by to talk with the chief, if ya don't mind."

Lockhart had just finished his second helping of food when Freddie walked in. He wiped his mouth, reluctantly pushed away from the table, and excused himself to the foyer.

"Don't be a stranger Freddie," Jill called after Lockhart and Freddie as they walked out the front door.

Freddie smiled. "Depends on whether or not yer willin' ta share your chili recipe with me."

Lockhart almost thought he heard a passive-aggressive twinge to Freddie's tone.

The two stepped outside, Freddie already with a fresh cigarette in his hand. The smell of his last smoke still hung in the air, and the cordial look he'd worn in front of Jill suddenly soured. In his other hand, he held a blank manila envelope.

"What's up Freddie?" Lockhart asked as he tried to pick a broccoli floret from between his teeth.

"Sorry to interrupt you, Chief. I tried to call, but you didn't answer."

Lockhart felt his pockets, realizing he must have left his cell phone in his room. "Sorry. What's in the envelope?"

"You got a fax from the FBI."

"A fax? We still get faxes here?" Lockhart quipped. "Isn't that some kind of blasphemy in the age of e-mail?"

Lind didn't pay attention to the comment. He looked nervous, and his eyes kept shifting across the ground, out of sync with his rocking from foot to foot.

"You read it already, didn't you?" Lockhart asked.

"Well, yeah…I mean, no, not intentionally…but, well, I didn't know it was important."

"Relax and take a breath," Lockhart told him, though he knew the FBI wasn't in the habit of sending faxes just for the heck of it. "What does the fax say Freddie?"

Deputy Lind took a seat on the porch swing and lit his cigarette. It was more reflexive than anything; his mind was clearly somewhere else, and he barely even took a puff. "They got a hit on the prints, Chief. They weren't Scott's."

Lockhart leaned back against the porch railing. It

was good news, but it didn't make sense that the FBI would send sensitive materials about an active investigation via fax, which was never confidential, even though the disclaimer to keep it that way was printed at the bottom of every page.

"They got a hit on the identity," Lind stuttered and took another short puff off his cigarette. "Guy was a soldier…" His eyes locked on the Crayton chief of police. "He's been dead for ten years."

Deputy Lind turned from his seat at the Bemidji FBI office and spoke to the back of Chief Darren Lockhart's head. "Are you sure about this, Chief?"

Freddie hadn't been easy to convince that going to the FBI as "outside investigators with knowledge of the crimes at the Witch Tree" was a good idea. He was definitely not happy that it was a paper-thin excuse that relied heavily on Lockhart making phone calls that Freddie wasn't privy to.

"Kind of a gray area, Freddie," Lockhart said without turning from his own computer monitor.

"That doesn't make me feel any better, Chief."

Lockhart stopped moving his mouse for a moment and turned an eye over his shoulder. "Scott Erickson, Freddie. Focus."

Deputy Lind chewed on a loose hangnail and flicked at his cigarette lighter just enough to create a spark before he finally conceded and turned back to his monitor.

"According to the coroner's report," Lockhart said as his eyes scanned across the computer screen, "the owner of our fingerprints, Steven Zito, died of a stroke in 2002, at the age of forty-nine."

Lockhart had no idea how he was going to link

fingerprints on the Ericksons' truck bumper to a man who'd been dead for a decade, but he had to look.

Freddie tapped a finger on his computer screen. "Got an obituary notice here from *The Los Angeles Times*."

"What's it say?" Lockhart asked as he turned to look over Freddie's shoulder.

"Uh, 'Steven Zito, forty-nine...survived by wife Anne and two sons, passed away Thursday after complications following a stroke...Vietnam vet...inspiration...'" Freddie paused his scan of the article and twisted his head to the side to stare straight at Lockhart, the whites of his eyes looking nearly double their normal size.

"What is it Freddie?" Lockhart asked as he scanned the article to see what had made Deputy Lind stop cold.

"'...despite the loss of his right hand in a car accident.' Jesus, Chief. You said those prints off the bumper were from a right hand. It's like something out of damn horror movie," Freddie said in a low voice. "What the hell is going on?"

CHAPTER 31

Agent Caitlyn Rhodes walked with strength, confidence, and purpose. Her shoulders were squared, and her posture was perfect. She was the picture of exacting detail, from her tailored, form-fitting suit to her perfectly pulled-back hair, not a strand out of place. On the outside, Caitlyn looked like the world was at her fingertips. On the inside, however, she was a clenched fist. She needed more to go on.

With only two days left, per dictum straight from Mount Olympus, to get headway on the Witch Tree case and no results on the DNA from the blood samples, all her hopes rested on the narrow shoulders of Nick Allen.

It seemed Caitlyn wasn't the only one dealing with issues. Instead of the normally buoyant and over-caffeinated Nick Allen she'd come to despise, she found a man glued to his computer, his brow furrowed as he typed rapidly and without pause at his computer.

Caitlyn gently knocked on the metal cubicle frame. She had never seen Nick working so diligently; until that moment, it had always seemed that he'd handled his job with an unnatural ease. She felt the nearly uncontrollable impulse to overlook his dozens of sexual advances and inappropriate comments and actually give the exhausted-looking guy a hug. "Nick?"

Nick Allen glanced up for just a moment. "Oh, hey, Agent Rhodes."

"Everything all right?"

Nick finally stopped typing and removed his glasses. He squinted as he pinched at the red divots that were indented in the bridge of his nose. "Yeah. Just been burning the candle at both ends. I got caught up working an identity theft case and wanted to make sure I worked on that second hard drive you brought in." He sounded professional, kind, and considerate, and Caitlyn assumed he had to be exhausted.

"I appreciate that, really. Did you find anything?"

Nick nodded and reached across the aisle to pull an empty chair over for Caitlyn to sit down at.

Caitlyn sat with a, "Thanks."

He gave her a timid, sideways smile. His eyes were dark in ways that even Mountain Dew evidently couldn't cure. Caitlyn wondered if he had gotten any sleep in the last two days.

"Well," he said, his tired eyes scanning across lines of code on his monitor, "the kid's not dumb. I found a few less secure files that look like he was trying to figure out how to hack the traffic signs. It looks like he wanted to warn people on 35 that there is a 'zombie apocalypse ahead.'" Nick scoffed. "That's not even original." He then pulled open a couple more sub-screens on his monitor. "The first hard drive you brought in was easy. On that one, only the Internet history was cleared. This kid used a Linux operating system. The files are compressed with tar compression and encrypted with GPG." Nick paused and turned his head toward Caitlyn. His look told her he was trying to see if she was following along.

"Keep going. I want to know it all," Caitlyn assured him. "So, you think he was just trying to keep stuff away from nosy parents?"

Nick Allen shook his head. "Maybe, but that'd be overkill, if you ask me. He was worried about outside users seeing his files too."

"What's in the files?"

"Not sure. We're still running the algorithm to try

and crack the password."

"How long will that take?" Caitlyn asked and looked at her watch.

Nick shrugged as he mulled the answer over. "Not sure about that either. Depends on how paranoid the kid was. Could be four hours, could be four days. Could be never."

"So we have nothing?"

"I didn't say that." Nick smirked. "You wanted me to explain it all. What we have are accessed files, ones that weren't ever saved on the hard drive."

Caitlyn wasn't anywhere near as tech savvy as Nick Allen, but she knew what that mean. "Like files from a flash drive."

Nick Allen nodded. "Yup."

Agent Rhodes nodded and immediately got on her phone to request assistance in a search of the Gillespie's house.

CHAPTER 32

Chief Lockhart's investigation was limited to looking into the disappearance of the Ericksons' truck, as it was related to the defacement of federally protected land. His use of federal files fell within the loophole of out-of-sight/out-of-mind. His connections with the Bureau granted him occasional favors and leeway; however, the use of federal resources for an investigation by a small-town police chief waded into the realm of illegal and prosecutable.

In hindsight, such things might have gnawed at Lockhart, but something was going on with the case, and he needed answers. If Scott was still alive, he didn't have time to spare. And even if he wasn't, his parents deserved answers.

Lockhart had sent Deputy Lind home hours prior, deciding there was no sense in both of them getting drowned in the waters of federal prosecution— especially for a paper trail that made as little sense as the one Lockhart was following.

How could the fingerprints off a L.A. man who's been dead ten years appear on the bumper of the Erickson's truck? The truck itself was just over ten years-old. All Lockhart could do was follow the paper trail, and sadly, there wasn't much of a trail there. Steven Zito's widow still resided in California, and she was of deteriorating health; her address was listed as a nursing home.

It had taken more than a few phone calls to actually get in touch with her, and when he finally did, she wasn't able to answer many of Lockhart's questions. She was understandably confused in regard to the questions about her late husband.

"Please, Mrs. Zito, I know this must be a very strange thing to hear, but I assure you, these questions are of the utmost importance." Lockhart's voice was a combination of haste and tenderness. He felt like he was prodding his own mother for information.

"And you say you are a police officer *where*?" Mrs. Zito's voice trembled with a sound like pebbles clicking together.

"Crayton, Minnesota, ma'am."

"I've never heard of Crayon, Minnesota.

"That's *Crayton*, ma'am."

"That either."

Lockhart suppressed a groan. "Mrs. Zito, is there anything you can tell me about the surgery on your husband's hand?"

"Steven had his hand removed," she said matter-of-factly.

"Yes, ma'am, but can you tell me anything more about that? Did anything go wrong with the surgery?"

There was a pause on the other end of the phone.

"Ma'am?" Lockhart asked with the assumption that she had hung up or had possibly just fallen asleep.

"Are you asking about the lawsuit?" she finally asked.

"Lawsuit?" Lockhart asked, baffled; he hadn't seen anything about a lawsuit connected to her husband's accident.

"Well, I'm not supposed to discuss the settlement..." she said hesitantly.

Lockhart could feel his heart beating as he held his breath, afraid that a door was about to be slammed in his face.

"...but to hell with those damned lawyers. Crooks, all of 'em. None of it'll bring my Steven or his hand back."

Lockhart released the air that had started to burn in his lungs as Mrs. Zito explained the malpractice lawsuit they'd filed after the removal of her husband's hand. The surgery and the subsequent amputation had been deemed unnecessary, given the extent of his injuries, and Steven and his wife had settled out of court for a cash sum.

"Uh," Lockhart managed as he processed the information, "do you happen to remember the name of the hospital or the surgeon?"

CHAPTER 33

"Wow! Now that's a lot of porn."

Agent Caitlyn Rhodes ignored Nick Allen's comment and went on with her review of the files they'd printed off of Brandon's hard drive. While he was right about the boy's penchant for pornographic sites, it did nothing to shed light on his disappearance or his connection to whatever had happened at the Witch Tree.

There was a knock at the conference room door.

"Agent Rhodes?" asked a young-looking agent wearing a blue FBI windbreaker. "We're all set."

He was a part of the additional search team Caitlyn had approved for the reinvestigation of Brandon's room.

"I'll be right with you," she said and turned to Nick Allen. "Keep looking through the files. We'll see what we can find in the house."

The idea had been to discover the missing flash drive that would allow Nick to access the partial computer files. The hope had been that those files would shed light on the investigation. Both hinged on actually finding something in the young porn addict's domain.

They had been outside of their authority at the initial interview with the parents, unable to actually search the house. The parents had given permission to take Brandon's computer, but that didn't come with the stipulation to search the rest of his room. Caitlyn rested her hopes on the cooperation of his parents and the additional resources for a break that she desperately needed. Fortunately, it seemed that two more days of no word from their son was all the motivation the

Gillespies needed to let the FBI search their house.

Two hours of searching yielded nothing. They had found more pornography, some marijuana residue in a desk drawer, and a few fireworks, but no flash drive. The futility of the situation began to set in like a leg cramp.

Agent Rhodes couldn't figure it out. *Maybe Brandon took the flash drive with him. Maybe it was a friend's. Then again, maybe we're just...wrong. Maybe there is no flash drive after all.*

Rhodes's eyes scanned the room halfheartedly for what seemed like the hundredth time. As her field of view drifted past the doorway, where Brandon's mother had been hovering, something clicked. Maybe the problem was that Agent Rhodes just wasn't capable of thinking like a teenager—or, more specifically, like a teenage boy.

"Mrs. Gillespie?" Agent Rhodes asked as she motioned for her to come in the room.

"Yes?" Mrs. Gillespie responded sheepishly.

"I was wondering if you might help us with something."

"How..." She paused. "How can *I* help the FBI?"

Rhodes sat on the bed as gently and demurely as she could. "You know, when I was a little girl, I had this hiding spot where I kept my diary or Halloween candy or other special things. It was just in a little space behind my desk, but I thought I was really sneaky and that no one knew about it. Well, one day, we were hit with a nasty rainstorm, and our roof started to leak. I can still remember the water stains from the leaking walls. I got home from school and was horrified to see that rain had leaked into my room, right above and around my secret hiding place. I ran over, praying that my diary hadn't gotten wet, but when I looked, it was gone. Then my mom came in and said, 'Don't worry, honey. I moved your diary when I saw the walls starting to leak.'" Caitlyn looked down, smiling at the old memory. "My mom had always known." She tiled her head ever so slightly and intentionally sympathetically up at Mrs. Gillespie, "Mothers *always* know, don't they?"

Caitlyn watched Mrs. Gillespie's eyes drift to the corner of the room. There was nothing there: no desk, no boxes, nothing. "I've seen Brandon over there before. I think the edgings are loose." Her voice was barely above a whisper, like a quiet breeze. "If I thought it was important, I swear I would have told you sooner."

Rhodes got down on her knees and pulled up the corner of the carpet, then pried away the edging where it met at the corner. Mrs. Gillespie was right: The nails were loose and slid right out. A small flap of carpet easily pulled away to reveal a small space in the wall, near the floor—a space just big enough to conceal a magazine...or a flash drive. In fact, there were several flash drives there in a Ziploc bag.

Agent Rhodes barely had time to thank Mrs. Gillespie on her way out the door.

"Well," Nick Allen said as he took a long swig of soda, "I can see why Brandon didn't want these files seen."

Only Nick Allen and Agent Rhodes sat in the file room, looking over the contents of the flash drives, as what they had found was a bit sensitive. It was an understatement for Caitlyn to say the pictures they scanned through were upsetting—not as an agent, per se, but as a woman.

Picture after picture of the same naked girl was splashed across the screen. In each one, her face was obscured or turned in some way. The sheer quantity was obsessive. It was clearly a fixation, but it was of little help. Pose after pose, file after file, it became ever more clear from dates on the files that the collection was something akin to a blitzkrieg attack: over 100 pictures had been snapped in a period of 14 days.

The girl's body was young, maybe eighteen, with creamy white skin and black hair that almost made her body glow. Her form was frozen, captured for all time in each pose. Every one was seductive: legs spread, breasts cupped, teasing, always teasing.

Agent Rhodes couldn't shake the feeling that it was wrong, and for reasons beyond the obvious. A single picture would have been one thing, but over 100 was something else. *Was it really just about sexuality? Exploration? Or was this taunting?* Whatever it was, she suddenly realized the identity of the mystery model lay not where the eye was drawn, but in the corner of a single shot. "There!" Caitlyn pointed excitedly.

"What? Where?" Nick Allen asked, having missed it completely.

In one picture, with the girl's face turned away, she was posed in front of an open window at night. Clearly, it was more teasing, even of passersby or neighbors. In that window hovered a specter of a face, and it was that face that had gotten Rhodes's attention. "That! Can you enhance that picture? I need to see who she is."

CHAPTER 34

On June 16, 1985, Dr. Alexander Johnson performed an amputation on the right hand of Steven Zito following an automobile accident. Mr. Zito had been involved in a collision when another driver failed to yield his right of way at a four-way stop and smashed into his passenger side.

While his body rebounded from the initial impact, Zito's arm struck the driver side door, breaking the ulna, the gear shift column collapsed on his right hand, crushing several bones. Dr. Johnson's assessment, without seeking a second opinion, was to remove the limb at the point of fracture.

The subsequent malpractice lawsuit resulted in a cash settlement for the Zitos, much to the chagrin of the hospital and Dr. Johnson; in fact, it was the surgeon's last time to ever don the mask and wield the scalpel. Prior to that, Johnson had been on staff with the hospital since the 1950s.

For the life of him, Chief Darren Lockhart couldn't figure out the connection between Johnson, Zito, and Scott Erickson. In fact, even finding information on Alexander Johnson was difficult. There were actually records for seven Alexander Johnsons in the Los Angeles area in the 1950s, and sorting through them was something of a hassle.

The real issue seemed to lie in the fact that prior to 1951, Lockhart could only find records for five of those men. He assumed two must have moved out of state, but finding so much as a trace of them would take weeks without better resources. To top that off, his own investigation into the matter was still off the books.

To add to the confusion, in 1950, one of the

Alexander Johnsons had been declared missing by his wife, but there was no record of that missing persons case being closed. There had been no follow-up with the wife, and Lockhart couldn't determine which officer had filled the report in the first place, not that they would be of much help some sixty years later anyway.

It was like looking at a pile of breadcrumbs and trying to make a trail out of them. Deciphering an important clue from arbitrary happenstance would be next to impossible.

Lockhart rested his elbows on the long stretch of mahogany at The Pit Stop and rubbed the palms of his hands against his eyes. Nearly all the sand had run out of the hour glass. It had been six days since Scott Erickson's disappearance. If the boy had been kidnapped, there was little hope of finding him alive, if at all. So there was Lockhart, left sitting in a bar, ready to ponder over a shot and a beer, trying to figure out an ice-cold fingerprint lead. Chief Lockhart was tired and sober, which would normally be expected at ten in the morning, but he was working to change that. While tired and tipsy were not mutually exclusive of one another, they sure seemed to coexist just fine in Lockhart's world.

Before Lockhart could order his usual, Deputy Lind rushed through the front door of with a wild, almost-frantic look in his eyes. "Chief!" he exclaimed far louder than needed in the small establishment.

Lockhart sighed. "What's up Freddie? You look like you found D.B. Cooper."

"Better than that, Chief," he said with a grin. "We found your Alex Johnson!"

To be more accurate, it was Joy who'd located the

missing surgeon.

Back at the Crayton police station, Deputy Freddie Lind scrolled through page after page of information on his computer screen. "So, we've been working all night, and we finally found something." Freddie pointed at the screen, as chipper as a person who'd just awakened from blissful sleep. "Dr. Alex Johnson was a doctor at United General Hospital in L.A. from 1951 to 1985, but the guy is like a ghost. He doesn't have a driver's license or any credit cards. He's about as off-the-grid as a guy can get. We even called up the hospital to see if there were any security records, like a picture on an I.D. badge, but they didn't start that until less than two months after Johnson was already gone."

"Which we thought was a little too coincidental," chimed in Joy, who seemed elated about her role in the investigation.

"On top of that," Freddie continued, "prior to 1951, we can't find his records, right?"

"Yeah," Lockhart agreed hesitantly, as he had no idea where his deputy was going.

"Well, it was Joy who came up with the idea that maybe he and the Alexander Johnson who disappeared were the same person."

"Okay, you two. Now you lost me," Lockhart said as he rocked back in his chair.

"What if someone stole his identity?" Joy asked excitedly.

Lockhart sighed. "More of a twenty-first-century crime, don't you think? Besides, before you all get too far down the rabbit hole on this one, let's not forget that the missing man was a doctor. Who steals the identity of a doctor, then performs surgeries for three decades?"

The deputy and police secretary stared at Lockhart blankly.

"Okay," Lockhart finally conceded, "go on."

"See, according to his résumé, Dr. Johnson was also a med school professor on the East Coast." Freddie proudly pulled up an archival picture from a graduating class alumni photograph. He pointed to a man who appeared to be in his late fifties. "That's him."

"Wait," Lockhart said as he leaned forward, squinting at the picture. "That guy was performing surgery for thirty-two years *after* this picture? He'd have been in his eighties."

Freddie and Joy exchanged grinning glances.

"Exactly," Joy said, "so we cross-checked the graduating class—all ten of them—and the staff."

"And?"

"And we found at least some kind of work history or fellowship or scholarship for each, all except for—"

Lockhart was all ears as Freddie cut in.

"A lab assistant named Henrik Werner."

"Kraut name if I ever heard one," Lockhart joked.

"Wait. There's more," Joy said, positively giddy with excitement.

"We couldn't find any record of a birth or death certificate for Henrik Werner. His name was on a class list in the 1940s, but after 1951..." Freddie said, leaving the end open for the chief.

"Nothing?" Lockhart concluded.

"Right. Zilch."

"Hmm. Interesting, but I'm still waiting for the payoff."

Deputy Lind furrowed his brow and typed "Henrik Werner" into a Google search engine.

Lockhart sighed at the sight of it. "Are you kidding

me? A Google search?"

Lind didn't answer but clicked on the second page of search results that showed the name "Henrik Werner" in bold font, under "Historical First Medical class of Faustheim University, 1835."

"So..." Lockhart dragged it out, trying to form his thoughts appropriately. "You think the guy who cut off Steven Zito's hand is, what, a 200-year-old medical student?"

"I...we..." Freddie started and immediately corrected, "think whoever did all this is linked to that name. Maybe he is a grandson or something; something that goes way back, serious grave-robber stuff and a pro to stay off the grid. There is only one Alex Johnson in the area, and it's a kid from Superior, Wisconsin."

"Or..." Joy said with a nudge into Freddie's ribs.

Freddie rolled his eyes and begrudgingly offered an alternative explanation. "Or else the guy is some kind of Frankenstein who steals body parts for his own weird experiments to extend his own life."

Lockhart had no words and just stared at his deputy, then at his secretary/landlord. Then he stood and stretched his arms, cracking his neck from side to side. For a moment, he debated just going back to The Pit Stop to start up where he last left off, but he had a job to do. "If I may play district attorney for a moment, what possible connection did you draw between a disappearance in Crayton, Minnesota, a possible act of violence at The Witch Tree, fingerprints from a man who's been dead ten years, and a guy who graduated from a German medical school in 1835?"

Blank eyes stared back at him, as though they had already explained themselves. Those same eyes also swam with childlike trepidation.

"Because to me," Lockhart continued, "it sounds as though you've connected the dots using whatever works of fiction you can think of. I'm a little surprised you didn't throw in some tacked-on curveball about time travel just to top it off."

Both Freddie and Joy looked hurt, and Lockhart immediately regretted his tone. It wasn't his intent to berate them, but he was tired and frustrated, and half-baked ideas were of no help to him. He eased himself back into his chair and rested his forearms on the desk. "Without a doubt, it has to be one of the dumbest theories I've ever heard, but..."

Both Joy and Freddie immediately perked up.

"...but that doesn't mean it isn't something to follow up on. Werner is the first name we've been able to find with any kind of connection that we can't explain. The fact that he more or less appeared from nowhere, possibly stole someone's identity, played surgeon for years, then stole someone's hand—"

"Not to mention that he just completely disappeared after the lawsuit. We tried to get information from the hospital, but all we could get was that he no longer did surgeries after the date of the lawsuit," Freddie added.

Lockhart paused to let all of it sink in. He debated the options that lay before him before eventually accepting the next course of action. "Are there any real estate agents in town?"

CHAPTER 35

Agent Caitlyn Rhodes would have preferred to do her questioning at the Grand Marais police station, but the mother of Stephanie Makowski, aka Raven, had refused to cooperate. So, once again, Caitlyn found herself surrounded by flowery paisley prints and a smattering of crucifixes. Again, she felt the cold stare from Raven and her mother, but this time, even without the help of Chief Lockhart, she had leverage, and she wasted no time in using it. "Tell me about Brandon Gillespie, Raven," she said.

"I don't know any Brandon," Raven said flatly. She sounded hollow, as if she were some kind of mannequin that simply had sound piped in through her mouth.

"Uh-huh." Caitlyn nodded. "Well, how about Vlad?"

"I don't know any Vlad either. Are you done?"

Agent Rhodes ignored the little brat and set a printout in front of her, an ad from an online bulletin board site that Nick Allen was able to retrieve from Brandon's hard drive. The ad was a request for a ride up to Grand Marais from Duluth the night of Scott Erickson's disappearance.

Raven's mother quickly snatched the piece of paper from the table for closer inspection.

"A day before the disappearance of Scott Erickson from his hometown of Crayton, this ad was posted by Brandon Gillespie, who, by the way, is also missing at this time. See, Brandon lives in Duluth, and being a teenager without a car, he seemed to be a bit stuck come time to actually make the trip to Grand Marais."

"So?" Raven asked, her voice finally carrying some semblance of emotion.

The girl wouldn't budge, and that frustrated Caitlyn to no end. She'd hoped Raven would give her something without her having to play her trump card, but she was done playing nice. Agent Rhodes walked to the door and asked one of the two local police officers to come inside from their place outside the front stoop. "Officer Lincoln, please place Ms. Stephanie Makowski, aka Raven, under arrest for conspiracy to commit kidnapping, obstruction of justice, as well as aiding and abetting a criminal."

"What?!" both Raven and her mother screeched in unison as Raven bolted to her feet.

Officer Lincoln stepped forward and repeated what Agent Rhodes had just said: "Ms. Makowski, you are under arrest for conspiracy to commit kidnapping, obstruction of justice, as well as aiding and abetting a criminal. You have the right to remain—"

Mrs. Makowski stepped in between the officer and her daughter, interrupting the Mirandas. "You have no right to come into my home and accuse my daughter of a crime. I told you she was with me the entire night. If you arrest her, I will sue your worthless little police force and the federal government. You have no idea what you're doing!"

Agent Rhodes never batted an eye. Instead, she just held up a single picture: a photograph of a young, naked girl, her face turned away. A frame of the picture was blown up in the corner of the sheet, revealing the face of Raven. She looked over her shoulder at the police officer. "Officer Lincoln, I will amend my statement. Please place Stephanie Makowski, aka Raven, under arrest for the willful creation and distribution of child pornography. She is seventeen years old, but it is my full intention to prosecute her as an adult and a sexual predator."

Raven's eyes swam and then started to dart back and forth between the officer, Agent Rhodes, and her mother.

"After inspecting the personal files of the missing Brandon Gillespie, we found over 100 pictures of your daughter in various poses and stages of undress. Under current laws, each picture is worth at least a year in federal prison. Unless…"

Raven clearly knew what Rhodes was alluding to, but she still offered a moment of protest in the form of a banshee-like scream, then tears and pouting that fell on deaf ears. Her own mother didn't move. Even when Raven physically reached out to her, arms extended for an embrace, Mrs. Makowski looked at her own daughter as if a hug were an alien act and pulled away from her touch.

Mrs. Makowski cleared her throat. "I would like to revise my statement. It appears that I was incorrect before. I must have been thinking of another night. My daughter was not with me on the night in question, now that I think about it." Now it was Raven's mother's eyes that looked cold and hollow.

"But, Mommy…"

It was almost a sad sight for Caitlyn to behold, but at that moment, she was overwhelmed with contempt for the person who'd singlehandedly obstructed her investigation. "Where are Brandon and Scott?" Rhodes asked quickly.

"I don't know," Raven said with a deflated whine as she crumpled into overstuffed paisley prints.

Rhodes nodded to the officer.

"No wait! Really, I don't know! I haven't seen them since that night!"

"So you *were* there?" Caitlyn asked; now full of her own loathing and contempt.

Raven nodded with her eyes to the ground, then explained it all. "The intention was to hold a Black Mass. The guy called Vlad, who I met on the Internet, was supposed to be some kind of expert or high priest or something. There would be four girls, four boys. Each girl was supposed to bring a boy we didn't really know—something about the mystery of it all or the lack of spiritual connection. But Shadow decided she was going to bring Scott, and I was...well, I was already, uh, texting with Brandon, so it was just easier to send him some naked pictures to get him to come along. He didn't want to, but it didn't take that much convincing after I started sending him those pictures. Vlad got kind of mad when he realized we knew each other, and he told us we would have to do the ceremony another time and that he needed to speak with the guys. He told us to go home and wait for instructions. He said he needed to cleanse them or something. He seemed pretty pissed off, so we did what we were told. Scott drove Shadow there, even though we girls were supposed to drive, so I gave her a ride home and we waited to hear more from Vlad, but I haven't gotten so much as an IM since you and that policeman showed up and started asking questions."

"Why didn't you tell us? You knew they were missing."

Raven started to cry. They weren't forced tears, the kind Caitlyn could only imagine Raven had practiced and honed during temper tantrums to get her way. These were real, her eyes swollen, a stuttered seizing her voice.

"He...Vlad told us not to. There was a plan, he said,

and parents and police would mess it up."

"What plan? You weren't concerned about leaving them there with a stranger, a supposed Satanic priest?"

"There were *four* of them—all guys. None of it was supposed to be real. It's just a game, to mess with people."

Caitlyn paced. She felt caged. "What's Vlad's real name?"

"I don't know. I only met him in person that night."

Agent Rhodes clenched her teeth in frustration. "What does he look like?"

Raven continued to sob and sniffle. Her eyes rocked back and forth in her head as she processed the question. "Um, he's about six feet tall, and he's got nasty scars all over his face." Raven traced a line around her jaw with her finger. "Like around here, like a mask. I don't know besides that. It was dark, and he was dressed in black. We all were." Her eyes swelled from crying.

Rhodes turned to the patrolman. "Get the description on the wire. I want it spread as far as you can, and send out an Amber alert on Brandon."

The officer stepped outside, cell phone to his ear.

The other officer came inside at the request of Agent Rhodes. With a nod, he moved over to Raven and pulled her to her feet.

"What are you doing? I cooperated!"

Caitlyn moved face to face with the teen. She'd clearly had enough. "You cooperated five days after a kidnapping and possible murder. You interfered with a federal investigation, young lady, and you better believe I will push every charge I can if those boys are anything but 100 percent healthy, you snotty little brat!"

All the while, Mrs. Makowski stood in shocked

silence. Even the pleading stare of her daughter as she was hauled away in handcuffs brought no reaction.

Caitlyn looked at her, waiting to see something in the form of emotion for what had happened or what was happening, but the woman seemed as black and emotionless as her daughter's thick eyeliner.

Just as Raven was taken to the door, Agent Rhodes stepped behind Mrs. Makowski, pulling back her arms and slapping on a set of handcuffs, which seemed to snap the woman back to reality.

"Wait…what are you doing?"

"Are you kidding me?" Caitlyn asked incredulously. "You lied to a federal agent to cover for your lying daughter. You're the poster-child for worthless helicopter parenting, and since you want to have so much to do with your daughter's fate, you get to share it. Enjoy prison."

CHAPTER 36

With a groan, Crayton Chief of Police Darren Lockhart crumpled up another piece of paper and threw it on the slow-building mountain around his trashcan. "No, that's not it either. It doesn't link up," he sighed.

Lockhart, Deputy Lind, and Joy had been sitting around the law enforcement office for over an hour, trying to track what was going on.

While Deputy Lind was convinced that Dr. Alex Johnson and Henrik Werner were connected through some kind of a strange body-snatching/illegal organ-selling operation, Joy had taken a more imaginative approach and believed Johnson and Werner were one in the same. Not only that, but she assumed Werner was some kind of modern-day Dr. Frankenstein who stole body parts and extended his life for an additional century.

"Could be necromancy," Lockhart suggested.

Joy and Deputy Lind looked back at him with no signs of following along.

Lockhart creaked back in his chair and rubbed the back of his neck as the memory faintly came back to him. It had been years ago, talking with an agent friend of his at a mandatory training excursion. Lockhart had been working a case in Detroit. The other agent, Herrera, had just gotten off a case where the suspect had been raiding fresh graves and taking body parts for use in magical ceremonies. Lockhart still grimaced at the thought of it. "Never mind," he said, not feeling like a trip down the road to lunacy.

The real problem Lockhart faced was the fact that while both scenarios sounded not only wrong but ludicrous, they also presented answers far more fully than anything else they'd been able to come up with thus far.

As the seconds ticked by on the antique cuckoo clock mounted next to the front door, their theories started to melt into a muddled mess of all kinds of strange theories that would have been better suited for a comic book. They really needed Shelly Fisher to arrive and shock a little reality back into their systems. Shelly was the only person in town, or closer than Bemidji, who had a license to sell real estate. Thus, she had accesses to residential information, as well as firsthand knowledge of exactly what to look for.

Lockhart wanted to find Werner. He couldn't shake the notion that Freddie had been right in at least some way that Werner was mixed up in all of it. Even more so, he believed Werner had actually taken the identity of Dr. Alex Johnson back in the fifties. He didn't believe Vlad and Werner were the same person, because the man would have been far too old for that to be believable outside the Marvel universe, but there were connections there somewhere. Lockhart found it far more likely that there was some kind of history behind the crime—perhaps a link to the Werner from the German medical school.

To what end, he had no idea, but basic searches for names like 'Johnson' and 'Werner' were basically useless. They needed someone who could find people—and not just people, but places. They needed to know if Johnson or Werner ever had any proximity to Minnesota.

Lockhart rocked back and forth slowly in his chair, doing his best to rub some of the tension out of the back of his neck. As usual, he was tired, more than a little frustrated, and ready to either find a lead or just chalk it all up to Scott Erickson running away. He was almost to the point of wanting to run away himself, truth be told. But he couldn't do either of those things. He knew that wouldn't be right, and he also knew there was more going on than they were able to see—yet.

The front door creaked loudly even before it was open enough to hit the entry chime. Lockhart, Freddie, and Joy all looked up expectantly as Shelly Fisher finally walked in the door.

"Hi, y'all," she said in her cheery, strangely Southern twang.

Joy had provided the back-story of Shelly having been married to some kind of a Southern gentleman not long out of college. She had lived on a Louisiana plantation for several years with him before what Joy only referred to as an "unfortunate divorce." After that, Shelly moved back home to Minnesota and brought her adapted Southern drawl with her. Now, twenty-some years later, it seemed to grow even thicker with every passing year.

"So sorry I'm so late, folks. I've just been busy as a dickens!" Shelly said, cell phone and day planner in hand. "I had properties up in Black Duck to show off to this nice young couple from Mounds View, then I had to go over—"

"It sounds like it's been one heck of a busy day," Lockhart interrupted, doing his best to avoid sounding condescending. "Thanks for making time for us. We're currently working on an investigation, and I was wondering if you'd be able to assist us with looking up some property listings."

A flash of agitation came and left from Shelly's face at being interrupted, but she remained very professional in her JCPenney pantsuit, her finger twirling at the long string of pearls around her neck. "Sure. What can I do to help?" she asked.

Lockhart rummaged through some of his papers to find the theory that sounded the least nonsensical. "Can you please look up property listings in St. Louis County for an Alexander Johnson?" He stood and offered his chair to her so she could work right there on his desktop computer.

Shelly accessed the real estate listings and began to cross-reference a search for Alexander Johnsons and St. Louis County homes for sale. Her fingers moved a mile a minute as she scrolled through screen after screen, but ultimately, she came up empty-handed. "I'm sorry. There's nothing under those search criteria."

"Is there any way we can look up a property owned or maybe purchased by an Alexander Johnson?"

Shelly looked back at Lockhart. "Chief Lockhart, I don't mean to be rude, but this isn't a magic box. I can't just make it tell me anything I want."

"Is there anything we can do?" Lockhart asked with his teeth firmly grinding away on his lower lip.

Freddie drummed his fingers on the desk. "Isn't there someone you can call, Chief? Someone with the Bureau?"

It wasn't a question Lockhart liked to address, aloud or otherwise, but it was fair given the amount of assistance he'd received under the table so far. "They aren't get-out-of-jail-free cards Freddie. The calls I've made are calls I can never make again."

The look was quick, and Lockhart almost missed it, but there was something between Freddie and Shelly— a faint lip twitch and reaction. Freddie's headshake was almost imperceptible, but it was there.

"What is it Freddie?" Lockhart asked, his own eyes

stopping Freddie before he had a chance to play dumb.

"Um," Freddie hesitated as time drew out, "I might know a guy who can help."

"Who?" Lockhart asked.

Freddie didn't answer.

"Freddie, whoever you can call, call them. Scott is out there somewhere. I know it. Trust me on that. But I also have a feeling time is running out for him and anyone else this maniac is messing with."

The look in Freddie's eyes was filled with pain, but he slowly nodded his head. "I do trust you, Chief, or else I'd never make this call." Freddie took out his cell phone and walked outside.

As soon as the door closed, Lockhart looked back at Shelly. "Who is he calling?"

Shelly looked back at him with an impassive face. "You'll have to ask him yourself."

Five minutes later, Freddie walked back in the office. His face looked drained of color, like he'd just made a deal with the devil himself. "Henrik Werner," Freddie said. "He lives in Minnesota."

No sooner had Freddie said it than Lockhart was racing to his car and on the phone with the FBI.

CHAPTER 37

Patrolman Martin Ortiz took his time in finishing his second cup of coffee. It had taken a few tries to get the color just right, and he savored every sip.

The lake blew a nasty gust of wind that time of year, and he'd spent all day ticketing vacationers who either didn't know or didn't care what the speed limit was along the North Shore Scenic Highway.

Waiting at home for him was his wife of just over a year, along with his newborn daughter. At only four weeks old, she still looked like some kind of a wrinkly peanut to him. All the baby books claimed she was still weeks away from smiling or even being able to actually see him instead of just a blur, and it was hard to feel the same kind of attachment to her that his wife had. *Maybe it's just easier for women to be mothers than it is for men to be fathers—or at least to feel like they are.*

Regardless, he loved his wife and his daughter more than he would ever actually let on to the other patrolmen. However, as much as he loved them both, he also cherished those small moments away when he could enjoy a hot cup of coffee just the way he liked it: a little cream and lots of pure cane sugar. He loved to wrap his hands around a fresh mug of steaming coffee and let the heat sink into his skins and cut through the Minnesota permafrost.

Of course, he would have enjoyed it a lot more if he could turn off his state patrol hand radio while he drank it. After three years on the job, it was mostly just white noise that he only noticed when his ears reflexively perked up to key words. The average person probably didn't hear more than just static.

So, Patrolman Ortiz was markedly surprised when

his waitress asked him a question. "What did he just say?" her eyes conveying a worried concern for such a young girl, probably not even out of high school.

"Uh...who?" Martin asked, looking over his shoulders.

"The radio guy. What did he just say about a suspect?"

"There was an Amber alert up in Grand Marais," Martin said, knowing exactly how much distance there was between he and Grand Marais, as well as how many other patrolmen were on duty between there and Two Harbors—not to mention who-knew-how-many local police.

"No, I mean the suspect. Did he say something about scars around his face? Like something you could get playing hockey?" The worried look grew on the young girl's face, and her hand trembled on the counter.

In that instant, it became clear to Martin that a slice of Betty's famous seven-layer chocolate pie and a refill were out of the question.

CHAPTER 38

"For the fifth time, this is Crayton Chief of Police Darren Lockhart. I need to talk with Agent Caitlyn Rhodes about the Erickson missing person case!" Lockhart was driving ninety through a maze of trees on a road he'd just discovered hours prior. Caitlyn had been right: There was a shorter way up to Grand Marais from Crayton, but it wasn't one that showed up on most maps. Freddie had keyed Lockhart in on his way out the door of the law enforcement office after hearing the news about a property listing for a Henrik Werner just north of Grand Marais. He only made one stop to grab his phone and back-up guns from the bed-and-breakfast.

"I'm sorry, Mr. Lockhart," the operator said flatly, "but as I said earlier, we are not permitted to divulge the location of agents in the field. I can take a message for Agent Rhodes and have her call you back if you like."

Lockhart had been driving at a demon's pace for over two hours, and it seemed like his way out of the trees would go on forever. A never-ending series of twists and turns made him feel more like Theseus trying to escape the Minotaur's Labyrinth than someone simply driving through northern Minnesota.

Lockhart's call-waiting beeped, and he hung up on the FBI operator. "Hey Freddie. What did you find out?"

"It looks like Werner's property is an abandoned factory. It's been out of commission since the sixties and went up for sale at a foreclosure auction. Werner bought it for cash, but that's the last place where his name appears."

"You know, Freddie, someday we're going to have to have a talk about exactly who you got this information from."

Freddie paused on the other end. "I know, Chief...but not today."

Lockhart thanked Freddie and hung up. He adjusted his vise-like grip on the steering wheel and gnawed nervously on his lip. He had no jurisdiction outside of Crayton and no probable cause to have the local PD raid the land. All he could hope for was Agent Rhodes getting his message and calling for backup. He couldn't afford to waste another minute, so for the time being, he had to take matters into his own hands, protocol or no protocol.

Going anywhere without backup wasn't just risky, it was stupid. Lockhart needed help, so he took a chance on some departmental cooperation from his new brethren in blue.

"Grand Marais Police. How can I direct your call?" answered the Grand Marais receptionist.

Lockhart's words came out hurriedly, as if he weren't still an hour out. "My name is Darren Lockhart. I'm the chief of police in Crayton. This may be a stretch, but two days ago I was interviewing a Stephanie Makowski, and—"

"Oh sure," the receptionist cut him off. "We just moved her and her mother to holding at Agent Rhodes's request."

Lockhart felt a twitch as he did a double-take at his phone. *Raven is in holding? What did Rhodes found out?* He decided to take a gamble. "Excellent, thank you. That's all I needed to know." Lockhart paused for hopefully added effect. "Oh, before I go, it looks like Agent Rhodes's cell phone died and she hasn't checked in. Did she leave any messages for me about where she's headed next?"

"Hold on. Let me check."

Lockhart felt sweat bead on his forehead as the muscles in his neck clenched in anticipation.

"No, none that I can see."

Lockhart's frustration came in a near wave of exasperation.

"At least not since she and Officer Wilson went back up to the Witch Tree to follow up on the suspect sighting."

Lockhart nearly lost control as he gunned the accelerator, pushing the car to over 100 MPH.

CHAPTER 39

Agent Caitlyn Rhodes moved slowly and purposefully through the trees. Her eyes scanned quickly back and forth between the shadows cast by the setting sun. Her hand was tensed, and her right shoulder drew slightly backward, her arm just clear of the gun on her hip.

Never once in all her time with the Bureau or with Dallas PD before that had Agent Rhodes drawn her weapon in the line of duty. Before leaving the patrol car with the officer from Grand Marais, Officer Wilson, she was pretty sure his name was, she'd checked the magazine in a sudden moment of panic, as if there might not be any bullets in her gun. She toggled the safety several times, just to make sure it was off. A round was chambered, and the clasp on the holster was left open, just in case.

The waitress from Betty's Pies had said a man matching the description of the one they believed to be Vlad had left with four gothic-dressed teenagers two nights prior. She had a hunch that the Witch Tree had something to do with Vlad's M.O. and that there might even be evidence of a fresh crime scene. *Is this Vlad really that audacious?*

Rhodes and Officer Wilson moved along without so much as a word between them. They shared the same air of tension. The moment had a pulse to it, and Caitlyn could feel it throughout her body. She felt a tightening at the base of her neck, and her breath came out shallowly, with anticipation of what she might find. *Maybe more candles. Maybe more blood. Maybe...a body.*

Through the clearing, Caitlyn saw that a body was

exactly what she'd found. Sitting on the edge of the cliff face, overlooking the water, was someone wearing a sweatshirt, the hood pulled up over his head. His hand rested gently on the trunk of the tree, as if he were stroking a beloved pet.

"You, on the cliff!" Wilson barked out. "Don't move!"

The figure obeyed and remained eerily still.

"This is protected land," Wilson added, his hand near his own holster. "What are you doing here?"

"Um…sitting?" the figure said as more of a question than an answer.

"Put your hands up!" Officer Wilson commanded as Caitlyn started to circle around to the side of the man.

"But you told me not to move," the man responded, his tone dry and matter-of-fact.

"Don't be a smartass…and don't make me tell you again."

Slowly, the figured pulled his hands from the pouch in the front of his sweatshirt and raised two leather chopper mittens in the air.

"Get up," Wilson continued, his hand now on the butt of his gun.

"I can't. My hands are in the air. I'll fall in the water."

Wilson grunted in displeasure. "Fine. Use your hands to get up, but do it slowly."

The figure stood up completely and slowly raised his hands back in the air.

"Now," Wilson said, inching toward him, "I asked you what you're doing here."

The man continued looking out onto the water, as unmoving as a statue. "I used to come here a lot with my father, back before this place was protected land. It was kind of our place together."

Wilson got within arm's reach. "You don't have anything in your pockets to stick me, do you?"

"No, sir."

Wilson patted the man down with one hand, up and down each leg, around his sides, and up his arms. "Take off the gloves."

"I have to move my hands then."

"Quit being a smartass and take off the damn gloves!"

Still slowly, the man moved one hand to the other and gently slid the glove off his right hand.

"Now the other," Wilson added, his eyes looking around the surrounding area.

Wilson's head was turned to the side, looking back at the woods, when the man pulled off his other glove. Caitlyn's eyes had never left the man, and as soon as the second glove came off, her hand was on her gun. Her mind was unable to fully compute what she saw, but she knew it wasn't right; it seemed impossible. Still, as quickly as she reacted, it wasn't fast enough. The man circled behind Officer Wilson and wrapped his arms around his head and neck. A quick jerk, and the echo of the man's spine breaking rattled through Caitlyn's very nerves.

Wilson fell in a heap at the hands of Vlad—hands that didn't match. One hand was stark white, almost hairless, while the other was slightly larger, darker in complexion, and covered in hair.

"Figured it out, huh?" Vlad asked casually, as if they were having a conversation at a bus stop—as though he weren't standing over the body of a police officer he'd just murdered.

Caitlyn's gun was raised, cross-hairs aimed right at Vlad's scarred face. "Get down on the ground!"

Vlad stepped over the body of Officer Wilson and toward her. In the span of two footfalls, Caitlyn quick-stepped forward, striking Vlad on the temple with the heel of her gun. His head snapped to the side, and blood immediately began to run down his face, but otherwise, he looked unharmed and unimpressed.

He dabbed at the blood on his cheek. "Are you kidding me? Do you know what a pain in the ass this is? The last one didn't work out so well either." Vlad rubbed the spot of blood between his fingers. "Oh well. Practice, practice, practice." Vlad pulled back his hoodie fully to reveal the line of scar tissue that ran around his face in a full oval from his brow all the way around his chin line. Just like Raven had said, it almost looked like he was wearing a mask. His sneer turned to a smile, and it wasn't until that moment that Caitlyn realized he'd cut her off from the forest and her back was to the cliff. "You know, it's not so bad," Vlad said, his voice almost a laugh. "Look at it this way. Maybe Gordon Lightfoot will write a song about you."

Agent Rhodes was over the cliff before she could even get a shot off.

CHAPTER 40

What followed was a jumble of images, muddled together by fear and adrenaline. The blow that knocked Caitlyn back from her footing felt like she'd been hit by a car. The kick to the stomach was strong enough to propel her backward, stumbling up the rock outcropping until her feet slipped out from under her and she slid off the edge of the cliff. As she tumbled over, in an act of sheer desperation, she was able to clamp her hand on a sharp piece of North Shore granite to stop herself from falling into the churning freezing water below. It was like holding on to a serrated knife, but it was better than the alternative.

Her eye level was below the ledge, and she couldn't make sense of the sounds she suddenly heard. It sounded like gunshots, but the blood coursing through her veins was deafening in conjunction with the slapping of waves against the rock below.

Agent Caitlyn Rhodes desperately tried to reach up for another rock to grip, but there was nothing. She knew she was going to fall, but then, despite it all, she didn't.

Instead, she felt a hand wrap around the sleeve of her coat at the wrist, and she looked up to see Chief Lockhart hauling her back up over the edge.

Crawling back onto the flat rock surface above, she could barely control the shaking in her body, but she still looked up to the cockeyed smile of Lockhart standing over her.

"I told you to call me if you needed a hand. So why didn't you?" he said with a smirk.

CHAPTER 41

Lockhart had arrived at the scene too late to stop the suspect from killing Wilson or knocking Rhodes over the cliff. He had gotten off two shots as the suspect disappeared back into the woods before he dove to pull Rhodes back up over the ledge.

Once Rhodes was safe and he had time to regret saying such a cheesy line in a heat of the moment, he went over and checked the downed officer's pulse, just to be sure. Wilson was indeed dead. Lockhart pulled out his phone and called it in. "This is Chief Lockhart with Crayton PD. We have a downed officer at the Witch Tree. Suspect is known only by the alias of Vlad and fled into the woods. Agent Rhodes and myself are in pursuit. Assemble all available units and meet us at the abandoned mill just past Mount Josephine on Highway 61." As he hung up he looked down at Rhodes, still frozen with fear. He wanted to let her be, but he couldn't. "Come on, let's go."

Rhodes looked confused. "Huh? Go where?" She looked at Wilson. "Leave his body?"

Lockhart did his best to tread lightly, but it still came out callous. "Yeah, I called it in. We need to beat Vlad back to the kidnapped kids. If they aren't already gone, he'll try to get rid of witnesses." He then extended his hand to Rhodes, who looked at it for a moment of confusion, like she had never seen a hand before. There must have been some kind of anchor in the gesture, because her face hardened, and she pulled herself back upright.

"How do you know where he's going?"

"It's complicated," Lockhart said as he looked around. "I'll explain as we drive."

The abandoned factory listed in Henrik Werner's name was about four miles away, and Lockhart had his foot on the floor the entire drive. Caitlyn called in for additional FBI backup with instructions to secure the building perimeter. Unfortunately, with the distance from the scene, it was also necessary to call in the request for state police and sheriff's department assistance in lieu of federal presence. They would need all the help they could get.

The factory was actually quite massive, given the listed square feet, and Lockhart balked at the idea of having to do a room-by-room search before Vlad was able to make it back. It had taken five minutes to make the drive, and even as the crow flew, there was no way Vlad could make the run in less than twenty minutes. The trees were too dense and the terrain too uneven for an ATV, but still, they were on the clock to get the building secured and search for survivors.

Lockhart stepped from his car and slid his gun from its holster with smooth reflex. Still dressed in his Crayton police uniform, he made sure his holster still sat on his hip as it always had as a federal agent. His finger rested on the trigger guard, and his eyes scanned from window to broken window for signs of movement. He took two steps closer to the building and gave a brief glimpse back at Rhodes, only to see her standing, empty-handed, beside the car. "Where's your weapon?"

"I don't know. I think it got knocked in the water when I went over the cliff ledge."

Lockhart squinted. "You think or you know?"

Rhodes's brow flickered, and her eyes scanned back and forth. "I'm pretty sure it did."

Lockhart ground his teeth together. "So Vlad could

be carrying your firearm?" Lockhart looked around again, scanning the trees. "Where's your backup?"

A blank stare gave Lockhart his answer.

He pulled the Kel-Tec back-up pistol from the holster on his left ankle and handed it over to Rhodes. "There're only seven shots, make 'em count."

Agent Rhodes took the gun and checked the chamber to make sure there was a round in the pipe.

As she gripped the gun, Lockhart noticed how hard she was trying to hide her nervousness. He was sure she hadn't done any entry training since the academy. "Breathe," Lockhart reassured her. "One of him, two of us."

Agent Rhodes took a long breath and let it out slowly through pursed lips. She nodded, and the two moved toward the building.

CHAPTER 42

Agent Caitlyn Rhodes was on edge: her arms, her legs, and her neck were all tensed to the point of being painful. She hadn't done a high-risk entry since her days with the Dallas PD, at least nothing with live rounds. Now she was about to enter an unsecured building with a former agent's small-caliber back-up piece, in search of missing teenagers who'd been abducted by someone capable of removing a man's hand and attaching it to his own arm. That was what she hadn't been able to put together back on the cliff. The hand was different because it wasn't his. That was also why there were different prints on the Ericksons' truck. It was Vlad all right—just not his prints.

Caitlyn's face soured as she scorned her own hesitation, but the truth was that she didn't want to be there. She didn't take any joy in the rush of the bust or the adrenaline of what might be around a blind corner like other agents. She just wanted answers. If it were up to her, they would wait for backup.

But there, not twenty feet away was the man who'd just saved her life. He moved with purpose and without hesitation. He was a good man and an excellent officer. He had the look of a man who couldn't be pulled away from the scene by anything less than a platoon of soldiers. She couldn't and wouldn't let him go in alone. For the moment, she *was* his backup.

Lockhart and Rhodes moved toward what appeared to have once been the front door to the factory, but as they got closer, something caught Lockhart's eye, and he nodded his head around the corner of the building. There, near the tree line, under a camouflage tarp, were the wheels of a pick-up truck with an attached trailer. It looked like a fresh coat of mud still covered the wheels of the trailer.

Lockhart motioned for Rhodes to move left, along the side of the building. He then nodded over to an open window that hung slightly ajar and moved parallel to Caitlyn and the wall, gun raised as he glanced inside.

Lockhart gave a slight nod to Rhodes and holstered his weapon so he could safely climb through the window. Once through, he drew his pistol again and motioned for Rhodes to do likewise.

Trespassing and *No probable cause* flashed in Agent Rhodes's head, but Lockhart never hesitated. He had briefly explained finding information that linked the owner of the property to Scott Erickson and the prints that were found on the Ericksons' truck—information that very well could match up with what Rhodes had seen with her own eyes at the Witch Tree. He had gone on about a man named Werner and a Dr. Johnson, but his thoughts had clearly been focused elsewhere on the drive and made little sense. He spoke like a man who was used to commanding, with disregard for whether or not everyone was following along.

Rhodes had faith in Lockhart's reputation; he had been a highly decorated agent and despite orders to the contrary, he had pursued the case on his own accord. In doing so, he had found a trail that had led him right to where Rhodes found herself, just in time to save her life. He was driven, if not reckless, but he was already inside the building; they were through the looking glass.

From the outside, the building seemed daunting enough, but inside it was even worse. Multiple levels of stairways and risers were covered with rows of massive, rusting machinery and debris that obstructed the view of the entire space. There was no way of knowing just by scanning the floor space how many rooms and offices were housed there.

"We need to split up," Lockhart whispered. "Take the stairs to the left and stay on an elevated plane. Backup should be here soon. We need to find the missing kids." He spoke with conviction, as if he was sure the kids were still alive. "If you see Vlad," Lockhart added as he turned to start his search, "don't mess around. Put a bullet in him." There was finality in his voice. He immediately moved away without hesitation, gun leading the way, scanning the floor of the factory.

Rhodes took another deep breath and moved up the nearby steps slowly, one step at a time, as though the ground beneath her wouldn't be there unless she tested it like hot bath water. Only a slight *click* came off the metal from contact with her leather shoes, but it sounded like an echo inside of Rhodes's own head.

Every shadow was Vlad. Every creak was his footsteps. He could have been anywhere, and that was what kept Agent Rhodes moving.

The stairs opened up to an elevated platform, an iron-grate observation level that had likely allowed supervisors to watch the activity on the production floor. At the end of the platform, about thirty feet away, was a glass-enclosed office with the windows painted black.

Rhodes held her breath as she turned the door handle. It groaned and clicked every inch of the way, until she felt the door start to slide free from the frame. The lights of the office were off, but the setting sun flooded in from one of the many windows on the main floor, illuminating the room.

Caitlyn suppressed a scream as she saw the body of what appeared to have been a young man, dressed all in black, splayed out on an operating table. His arms hung lifeless over the side of the table.

Around the body, in a variety of different cages and bondage, were four other teens, all begging, pleading, and reaching out for help, but Rhodes had difficulty focusing on their cries. She couldn't take her eyes off the body. She didn't feel the need to check for a pulse.

He wasn't moving...and his face had been removed.

CHAPTER 43

Lockhart felt like a federal agent again. Gun drawn, he searched room by room for anyone who might be held hostage by a maniac. Except he wasn't an agent; he wasn't even wearing a suit. He never thought it would happen, but the idea of changing from his police blues to a suit had never once occurred to him as he'd raced from Crayton. Lockhart's only thought was finding Vlad.

Lockhart wasn't really sure who Vlad was though. He was clearly too young to be Dr. Alexander Johnson, the man responsible for removing Steven Zito's hand twenty-five years prior. Still, he was linked to a property owned by Henrik Werner, or some relation thereof—a man who, for all intents and purposes, should have been dead a century ago, long before the property was ever purchased. He didn't know how it was possible or even if it was possible at all, but the man might very well consider himself to be some kind of modern-day Frankenstein. The fact that he was kidnapping teenagers en masse meant his delusions of grandeur were of epic proportions, and he needed to be stopped.

Each room Lockhart cleared was both a shot of adrenaline and a small defeat. He couldn't find anyone. There was no sign of life, yet all around him hung the air of death and decay—or so he thought.

There was just nothing there. It was just an empty warehouse. It was expansive enough that he had no idea where Rhodes had moved off to. The place was stale, and most of the machinery was completely rusted over. The floor was covered in wildlife droppings, and there were remnants of bird nests in the rafters.

Lockhart's mind slowly started to accept the

realization that he'd been wrong. He wanted so badly to get answers for the Ericksons that it had clouded his judgment. The trail was a figment of his imagination, pieced together by a small-town cop, his deputy, and their spunky secretary, like some bad seventies cop show. What he had secretly hoped to be his moment of redemption after his exile to backwoods Minnesota had quickly turned to his downfall. He had failed. The suspect would never return there, assuming that he'd ever been here in the first place. And to make matters worse for the disgruntled police chief, he'd opened himself up for trespassing, as well as a slew of federal charges.

Maybe worst of all, at least to Lockhart, was that he finally had to accept that Scott Erickson was gone. *It's all been for nothing. God. What am I gonna tell those poor people?*

Lockhart's gun lowered, and his shoulders and arms started to wilt with resigned acceptance. With defeat clear and present on the horizon, life, as it is prone to do, showed that Lockhart didn't have all the answers.

Maybe it had been that he was so focused on finding signs of life that he hadn't taken notice of the machinery covered in tarps. It wasn't so much that they were covered as the fact that some of the tarps, while still old and stained, had no dust or other debris on top of them.

Lockhart lifted up the corner of one of the tarps and saw the near shine of the matte-gray metal surface. It was an autoclave. *Wait. They use these to sterilize surgical instruments. What's this doing in some outdated factory among all these relics?* Next to it was another contraption that looked like a bypass machine.

There was barely a sound as Lockhart drew his Glock again.

Further down the production floor, in the corner of the factory, he saw a set of stairs leading down into a sub-basement, where a light was on. It was a faint glow, and Lockhart couldn't see it until he was less than ten yards from it, but it was there, hanging on the wall—a lone utility light that illuminated the stairway.

Lockhart spun to look for Rhodes, but she was nowhere to be seen. Gun forward, Lockhart moved down the stairs as fluidly as water rolling over stone. At the base of the stairs, around the corner, was a heavy, steel-plated vault door that looked like a holdover from the twenties. The door sat ajar, and inside, Lockhart saw a sight he would never forget: the drawn and emaciated form of Scott Erickson.

His leg was shackled to the metal gurney he lay on top of, IV drips hanging all around him. His left hand, or where his left hand had been, was now only a bandaged stump stained with dried blood.

Lockhart holstered his gun and rushed to Scott's side. "Scotty? Scotty!" He gently shook the boy by the shoulder, but he got no response. Lockhart placed two fingers on the boy's neck and checked for a pulse. "Come on, Scotty. I know you're still here. It's Chief Lockhart. Please, Scotty…"

The pulse was faint, but present, and Lockhart only had a moment to breathe a sigh of relief before his mind switched gears into keeping Scotty alive. He pulled out his cell phone but got no reception through the metal plating in the basement. "Damn it!" Lockhart snapped and looked back down at Scott.

Slowly, so slowly, Scott opened his eyes. It was barely a squint and done with the effort of a newborn baby, but Lockhart saw Scott's tired and scared eyes staring back up at him.

"Scotty, I have to leave you. It'll only be a second. I need to call an ambulance. I promise I'll be right back."

Scott slowly raised his left hand and reached out toward Lockhart. Lockhart took the hand that looked so pale and small in his own. There was almost no strength left in the poor boy, but the faintest squeeze of a grip and a tear rolling down his cheek broke the veteran investigator's heart.

With new resolve and energy from a higher purpose, Lockhart ran, two steps at a time, back to the main level, his hand reaching for his phone again.

At the top of the stairs, he stopped so quickly that he nearly stumbled over. Vlad stood less than twenty feet away, and he was pointing Agent Caitlyn Rhodes's gun straight at him.

The man—Vlad, Henrik, or maybe even Dr. Alexander Johnson himself—just stood there, one hand around the gun, one nestled in the pouch of his hooded sweatshirt. The hood was pulled back, and Lockhart could clearly see the ring of scar tissue around his face. The gash on his temple had a line of dried blood underneath it. He had Lockhart dead to rights, but he didn't shoot. He just stood there, with his gun leveled at Lockhart's chest. "Slowly take the gun from your holster with just two fingers and toss it down the stairs," Vlad commanded.

Lockhart did as he was told, and his gun clanked down the iron stairs, clattering to the landing below.

Vlad looked him up and down with probing eyes. "Backup?"

Lockhart lifted his left pant leg, revealing an empty holster; he had given his back-up piece to Rhodes.

Vlad smiled and looked at the gun in his hand. "She forgot her backup, huh?" He paused and looked coldly into Lockhart's eyes. "Do you know who I am?"

"Yes, Vlad."

"Do you know who I *really* am?"

"No," Lockhart admitted. "I have no idea who you really are."

Vlad shrugged. "It doesn't really matter. I've had plenty of names over the years, and I'm sure I'll have plenty more."

"A name like, say, Frankenstein?" Lockhart wagered.

Vlad let out a single loud "Ha! *Frankenstein...*" Vlad's voice trailed for a moment, and a hint of a German accent suddenly became clear. "An inspired fiction work, quite brilliant actually. It was a glorious time to be alive. Back then, there was so much to discover about the human body, so much taboo and forbidden, but science could not be impeded." Vlad squinted for a moment, and Lockhart braced himself for the bullet he was sure was coming. "It took pioneers, sacrifices." Vlad turned his hand, showing the unmatched tone between the skin on his hand and forearm, clearly divided by scar tissue. Then he pulled at the side of his hood, revealing his collar and what looked like small metal implants in his skin. "Science— *true* science—requires sacrifice. For that, I am rewarded."

Lockhart stared at him, unfazed, but filled with sudden contempt. "What sacrifice? What reward? You kidnapped kids and cut them up. You're no scientist. You're nothing but a sick freak."

Vlad sneered and pointed the gun back at Lockhart. "I *harvest*. Through me, they shall be immortals in history. Their lives pale in the scope of what I have achieved. I am as close to perfection as we have ever come."

"Not from where I'm standing," Lockhart goaded. "You look like a poorly done patchwork quilt—and you're a monster."

"History is written by the victors, and the victors are those who survive long enough to retell the world as they made it."

A new voice suddenly came from directly behind Vlad. "You'll have plenty of time to work on your survival skills in prison."

Vlad's eyes widened at the sound of the gun cocking behind his head, where Agent Rhodes stood.

"You're under arrest for kidnapping, torture, and murder."

The accent left Vlad's voice. "I'm impressed. It's been a long time since anyone's gotten this close to me or my work. Too bad it won't end the way you think it will."

"Shut up," Rhodes demanded, the stress in her voice palpable. "Drop the gun and *slowly* take your other hand out of your pocket."

Vlad didn't move.

"I *will* shoot you," Rhodes assured him.

"Then we all die," Vlad said and eased his hand out of the pouch to reveal a handheld metal device that looked like a small flashlight. With his thumb, or maybe a stolen one, he was holding down a small plunger on the top. "Do you know what this is?"

"I do," Lockhart said, his mind flashing to the last time he'd seen a pressure-sensitive explosive trigger. If Vlad's thumb came off the trigger, it would radio-activate explosives that could have been planted anywhere around them.

"Do you really think I would do all of this just to let my work fall into someone else's hands? Do you think I have done what I have done for so long that I'm not ready for a pesky little interruption such as this?" Vlad had the sneer of an animal protecting his territory. "So I hope we all understand that if I die, I'm not going alone."

Lockhart didn't move. He didn't doubt for a moment that the man was insane and that his resolve to his goal was clear, regardless of whether or not it was some kind of bluff. Until that moment, Lockhart had relied on Agent Rhodes as his sole backup and never considered a bomb. There were oxygen tanks near Scotty, and if there were other teens around, there was no way to know how much explosive material was littered around the area. They were at a stalemate, and Lockhart needed to take a chance. "You won't do it. Deactivate that device."

Vlad raised an eyebrow. "A negotiator as well? Hmm. I'm duly impressed. I thought the feds around here were nothing more than desk jockeys these days."

"I'm not a fed. I'm the Crayton chief of police."

Vlad smiled a wide grin that seemed prompted from a second thought. "I like Crayton. I always have." Dark circles grew beneath Vlad's eyes. "That bitch didn't listen to me. Neither of them did. I told them to bring strangers, no links. So hard to get men to come to me, but they will follow some little skirt off a cliff— sometimes literally." His eyes trailed down to the hand holding the device. "I went through a lot to make sure you stopped looking for him."

Lockhart saw that the madman wasn't going to back down, but he knew if Vlad's intention had been to kill them all, he would have already done it. "Why don't you just leave? Go somewhere else? You're the one with the bomb."

Vlad shook his head. "I like it here. I've been around, believe me. I liked Nashville, too, but this place is mine." Vlad cocked his head to the side. "You know what? You look healthy, about my size..." Then Vlad turned and looked over his shoulder at Agent Rhodes, the gun just inches from his head, and eyed her up and down, like a hungry dog gawking lustfully at a steak. "Then again, times change. I should be more open to new experiences."

Lockhart shifted his weight forward, ready to make his move, thinking he might be able to get to Vlad fast enough to get a grip around the trigger.

Just then, the flashing red and blue police lights burst through the factory windows.

Vlad's face twisted, the lights casting eerie reflections on his disgusting scars. "Ah, to hell with it."

CHAPTER 44

Officer Wirth slowly rolled his police car up to the abandoned logging factory just outside Grand Marais. He was conflicted with feelings of annoyance and curiosity. He was supposed to be off his shift ten minutes earlier, but he'd suddenly gotten called in. Some police chief from out of town was requesting assistance.

Even the Cook County sheriff's office and state police, with the sheriff's office acting in support of the state, got the call, and since they were located in Grand Marais as well, they had gone to another location to follow up and assist while the Duluth FBI would be over an hour out, even by helicopter.

Just trying to follow all that information was enough for Wirth to be intrigued, so he didn't bother arguing via his police radio—at least not too much of an argument. It was more excitement than he had heard on the box in a long time.

As far as Wirth was concerned, it was more than likely being blown out of proportion, and he was sure none of it could actually be as bad as they were making it sound. After all, it was Grand Marais. Ever since those rumors of a missing kid out at the Witch Tree had gotten out, gossip had been swirling around about all kinds of unexplained events. Sure, that creepy goth girl and her mom had been taken into custody by the FBI lady, but he didn't think it was really necessary for him to go check out a factory that no one had used for decades. It sounded like the action was wherever the sheriff deputies were at.

It really wasn't that much out of the way for him to at least take a look around the property, though, and when he saw the Crayton police cruiser parked out front, he considered that there might actually be something to do. He only hoped it wouldn't result in a pile of paperwork, which was his biggest pet peeve about working for the police.

"Car Four checking in at the old Victoria Factory," Wirth reported into his radio. "Any word from whoever called in the first report?"

Brief static from the radio followed for a moment, then a crackle, "Negative, Four. No additional contact with caller."

Wirth sighed and eased himself out of his car. He leaned on the open doorframe. "What about the sheriff's office? Where are they?"

The radio again filled with static, this time far more prolonged. "Sheriff's office has been instructed to maintain radio silence."

Wirth looked at the factory. "What? By whom?"

"The FBI has officially taken over the investigation."

Damn feds. Shaking his head, Wirth walked around the front of the car with his hands on his hips. He looked up at the factory in all its decrepit glory. The structure had been standing there as long as he had been alive, unused just as long. As a kid, Wirth and his friends had played around the factory, but never inside the place, for it always seemed too scary. It was a common place to come up with ghost stories and rumors, and there were constant dares and double-dog dares to walk closer to it. Even the teens didn't go inside to drink or smoke.

Wirth clicked his radio back on. "Radio, I'm on the property, but I don't see any—"

BOOM! He was cut off by all the windows of the factory being blown out at the same time.

CHAPTER 45

When Vlad released his thumb from the trigger detonator in his hand, every window in the building blew out from the resulting shockwave. All around had been a series of explosions, strong enough to knock Rhodes and Lockhart to the ground, but nothing close enough to have done serious damage.

Lockhart groaned as he tried his best to get back to his feet, but he felt like he had just taken a right hook to the temple. His eyes were blurred, and his equilibrium was completely thrown off. He could make out Rhodes twenty feet away, down, but stirring. His eyes started to clear just in time to see Vlad scurry across the factory floor.

Lockhart heaved himself to his feet. "Rhodes, get Scotty downstairs and out of here before the whole building comes down!"

Rhodes rolled over and gave a weak wave. "Other kids…" she coughed, but waved him off again. "Go! Don't let him get away."

The Crayton chief of police took off at a lumbering run, adrenaline flooding over his aching body. He could see Vlad weaving around debris ahead of him, and he refused to let the monster get away.

Upstairs, across platforms and the catwalk, Vlad ran full speed across less-than-stable surfaces like a man with purpose; that purpose was right behind him. For just a moment, Vlad looked over his shoulder and made eye contact with the closing Lockhart, and it looked as though Lockhart might actually catch up to the maniac. The catwalk ended, and there was only a series of windows that hadn't been partially blown out by the explosion, grinning like a row of broken, jagged, razor-sharp teeth.

But Vlad didn't so much as slow down. Rather, he ran, full bore, through the broken windows, the shattering glass flashing against the sky like diamonds.

Lockhart pulled up to the end of the catwalk and looked down twenty feet to the ground below. There, surrounded by broken glass, Vlad rolled across the ground, stopping facedown like a ragdoll. He slowly started to come up to his hands and feet. Lockhart looked around desperately, but there were no officers on that side of the building. *Where the hell is our backup?*

Lockhart clamped his teeth together and smacked the railing in frustration. "Damn it! Damn it!" He ran about halfway back down the catwalk and saw that the only readily visible doors to the factory were on opposite sides from where Vlad was. With a grateful heart, he saw Rhodes carrying Scotty, arm over her shoulders, from the building, with several other teens trailing behind her. Scotty was moving on his own power, albeit just barely.

Lockhart looked back to the window and realized he had no choice. With a couple loud grunts to motivate himself to do what he knew was stupid, Lockhart pushed off as hard as he could and hit the edge of the window as quickly as possible. For just a moment, he felt totally weightless, as if his feet would never touch the ground.

The intention had been to do his best to roll once he hit the ground. The reality was that as soon as his foot made contact, it folded underneath him, twisting his body in an unnatural contortion and slamming him into the ground.

Vlad was already crawling away, and Lockhart

hadn't jumped nearly as far as he thought he would. Lockhart's eyes lolled in his head as he watched Vlad slowly start to crawl away and felt powerless to do anything about it.

At that moment, maybe more than any other moment in Darren Lockhart's life, he wanted to give up. No matter how close he was to Vlad and catching a kidnapper, he was spent. His body felt broken, his mind exhausted. The act of standing or even moving felt like too much. Rhodes had Scotty and was no doubt calling in additional help from police—help that should have already been there. Scotty was safe, Rhodes was safe, and Lockhart was...done.

Slowly, Lockhart rolled over. His eyes, if for no other reason than chance, caught sight of Vlad. He had pulled himself to his feet and was braced against a tree. His face had been sliced up badly by the crash through the glass, but he was standing and still breathing, despite it all.

In that moment, Lockhart saw Vlad for the first time as what he really was: a monster. He knew if he got away, he would never stop. More kids would disappear and die, be that in Minnesota or some other unfortunate place. Lockhart couldn't let that happen. He was too old and had seen too many innocent people killed, and he would have rather died than live with the knowledge that he could have done something, no matter how futile, to stop a madman.

Once he set eyes on Vlad, he didn't move them as he forced himself to stand out of sheer, indomitable will. Breathing hurt, so he was sure his rib was probably broken. He could barely stand on his twisted ankle. His head felt cloudy, and he was barely able to hold a thought beyond primal, evolutionary reactions. At that moment, it was all about pure animal rage.

Vlad's eyes seemed to sink in disbelief that Lockhart was still standing. He stumbled from the tree and started to run again.

"Vlad!" Lockhart yelled and started his limping, grunting run after him.

Through the woven web of trees, the two men were locked in a chase that stood outside of time itself. The world melted away, and it was just the two of them—hunter and hunted—each man bumping from tree to tree, doing his best to gain ground on the other. At times, each man looked as though he were getting the better in a chase that felt eternal.

Eternity ended in front of an infinite expanse of blue.

Vlad had run back to the water's edge of Lake Superior, and Lockhart saw it. He moved to lean against a tree and pulled the back-up Kel-Tec from his right ankle holster. For only the second time in his life was he relieved at his over-preparedness. Vlad still had Rhodes's gun in his hand, but it was pointed at the ground as he looked out onto the water. Not far, just off in the horizon, the Witch Tree stood against the backdrop of the nearly-set sun.

"You know," Vlad said, looking off toward the Witch Tree, "there was a time when it was a lot easier."

Lockhart ignored him. "Drop the gun."

"The Ojibwe didn't see a difference between scientific and magical. Sometimes people just disappeared, and it was a matter of the bad spirits." Vlad laughed at his own sick inside joke.

"Drop your gun and get down on your knees."

Vlad wasn't listening either. He sighed loudly over the lapping of water near his feet. "Times change, and

I've done my best to change with it, to carry on the legacy, but maybe it's time to move on."

Lockhart cocked the hammer on his gun. "Drop the gun and get down on your knees. You are under arrest for kidnapping and murder."

Vlad swayed a little. The gun in his hand moved from side to side as he looked down at it, held by the hand that had belonged to Steven Zito. "You know, this was a gift as well as a birthright." One eye peered over his shoulder at Lockhart, right down the barrel of his gun.

"If you turn around without dropping that gun—"

Vlad blinked slowly and tested Lockhart's resolve.

One shot rang out as Scott's kidnapper turned to face Lockhart. The shot landed flush on Vlad's left shoulder. The man stumbled backward but did not fall and did not drop his gun. The dried blood on his face from all the glass wounds, mixed with sweat from his brow, created a sort of red death mask that was oddly less disgusting than his regular face.

Again, Vlad stepped forward, and again Lockhart fired, striking Vlad in the right thigh, dropping the man to the ground with little more than a groan. Still, the gun remained in his hand. "Don't make me kill you." Lockhart exhaled with total conviction in his voice.

Vlad smiled through the pain of two bullet wounds and extensive facial lacerations and raised his gun at Lockhart.

One more shot rang out and was silenced quickly by the frightened screams of seagulls hovering in the air, fighting against the cold North Shore wind.

CHAPTER 46

Agent Caitlyn Rhodes stood at the door of the ambulance, watching paramedics load the stabilized body of Scott Erickson in, while Cook County sheriffs appeared around the corner of the factory; they each had an arm hooked under Crayton Chief of Police Darren Lockhart and helped him to the nearest police car. He looked exhausted. His eyes were nearly closed, and for as little as he was actually moving, he could have been sleepwalking.

Caitlyn opened the door for him to sit down. "Are you okay?" Caitlyn asked as Lockhart when he slumped in the seat.

Lockhart's head sort of lolled to the side, and he looked up her slowly. "For the first time in years, I really could use a cigarette."

"Sorry. I don't smoke."

Lockhart smiled weakly. "How about a beer then?"

Rhodes stood up straight. "Lockhart?" she asked.

The police chief looked up at her. "Yeah?"

"Sit there and shut up. The paramedics will be over soon to check you out." That said, Rhodes turned to walk away when she felt Lockhart's hand on her wrist. She looked back and saw a look of genuine concern on the former agent's face.

"Scotty?" he asked.

Rhodes gently put her hand on his. "The paramedics say he's lost a lot of fluids and his body is in pretty bad shape, but it sounds like the kid's gonna pull through. He's being rushed to the Cook County Hospital. I've put in a call, and we're rushing up a specialist from St. Luke's in Duluth. Don't worry. He'll be taken care of."

Lockhart closed his eyes again and turned back in

his seat, his body sort of melting into the interior, as if, first time in his life, the strain was finally released from his muscles.

Caitlyn walked back to the factory. Dogs and officers were patrolling around the perimeter for additional explosives or bodies.

The four other teens, including Brandon Gillespie, that she'd been able to get out of the factory were huddled together, shivering in blankets as an EMT checked them out and the sheriff took their official statements.

The girl was from the group at Betty's Pie, as was the kid whose face had been removed. Their other two friends were unaccounted for, and she said she hadn't seen them since they all went to the Witch Tree. Her story matched up with Brandon's. After the supposed ritual, Vlad had taken them down one by one. The statements were all the same: "He was super strong and super fast." The rest was a hazy blur, so Agent Rhodes had to surmise that they'd been drugged.

Caitlyn wondered about the bloodstain that had been left on the rock, only to be seen the next day by David Crowe. Scotty didn't have any wounds to speak of, other than the removal of his hand, so she guessed the blood had to belong to one of the other boys. *Maybe someone resisted and actually did get lost in Lake Superior. Maybe Vlad intended to leave the blood, thumbing his nose at the world he considered himself to be a god of.*

Rhodes put a call in to her supervisors to appraise them of the situation and to get an update on the ETA for additional agents on the scene. It must have been the first time in who-knew-how-long that she did something even vaguely familiar to her, because suddenly her entire body felt exhausted. The adrenaline dump hit her hard enough that she could never remember a time when she wanted to crawl into bed more.

When Caitlyn finished her call, Lockhart was being checked out by paramedics, wincing in pain every time they even lightly touched his ribs.

"Well, I don't think they're broken," said the paramedic, "but they are sure bruised—maybe even cracked." He looked down at Lockhart's ankle as well. "And your ankle's twisted. Still, you're pretty lucky, buddy—all in all, I mean."

Lockhart snorted a weak, desperate sound and winced again with a twist, clearly feeling it in his ribs. "Doesn't feel too lucky to me. Hurt like hell running on it."

The paramedic looked back at Rhodes, then at Lockhart quizzically. "You *ran*? That's interesting," he said in disbelief.

"Why?" Lockhart asked.

The paramedic snorted. "Son, you're either crazy or stupid."

Caitlyn smiled and decided to chime in. "A bit of both, I think."

The paramedic stood up and walked back to the ambulance to get some bandages and a brace for Lockhart's ankle.

Caitlyn looked down thoughtfully at Lockhart. She wasn't a fan of kicking anyone while they were down, especially after he'd just gone through so much to find Scott and capture Vlad, but it had to be done. "I just got off the phone with my superiors."

Lockhart had closed his eyes again and leaned back in his seat. He didn't bother to open his eyes for the answer. "They want a debriefing, don't they?"

"It's procedure, Darren—protocol."

Lockhart groaned softly as he turned to face Rhodes once again. "There's gonna be hell to pay."

Rhodes didn't know what to say; she wasn't sure there were any right words. There had already been questions about how Scott's fingerprints—not to mention most of the townspeople's—had been in the system, but Caitlyn was sure there'd be far more indiscretions than the Boy/Girls Scout fingerprinting conundrum to contend with. Lockhart was yet to fill her in about how he'd even found Vlad's property.

There didn't seem to be a scenario in which Lockhart would come out of the whole thing unscathed, but Rhodes would do everything she could to make sure his actions would be known to the fullest extent for the review board.

Caitlyn left Lockhart in the paramedics' trusty care and walked back to the factory. The sheriffs had cleared the scene of explosives, and she walked gently through the scattered debris of twisted metal and broken glass.

She had been able to save Scotty, Brandon, two other boys, and a girl. If she were to take David Crowe's word about the crime scene, that meant there were two other boys still unaccounted for. She tried not to think about what might have happened to them. Their bodies had not yet been recovered in the building. *Maybe they got away. Maybe they had never been brought to the factory in the first place. Or maybe...* Caitlyn shuddered to think what the sick freak might have done to those kids and countless others over the years.

As she looked around the relics of a former industrial time, Rhodes felt no nostalgia. She looked forward to the idea of the building being torn down and plowed over, to rid the world of any remnant that might still exist from the evil that had lived there. With a little luck, or maybe some kind of justice, the memory of the place would be erased from the collective memory of time itself. The least humankind could do was to demolish the hell and hope it'd be forgotten.

As she walked out the door of the factory again, it saddened Caitlyn to realize that justice like that doesn't exist.

CHAPTER 47

Crayton Chief of Police Darren Lockhart sat alone in Dan's Café. The café, which was normally bustling at night, was empty at two in the afternoon. Head Chef and Town Deputy Freddie Lind hung the "CLOSED" sign in the door to give Lockhart a little time to himself.

A cup of coffee sat cooling in front of him, and the remnants of Freddie's BLT with avocado and garlic aioli sat on a plate to his side. He could have been asleep sitting up, for all anyone knew. He was focused on nothing in particular—just kind of sitting and staring.

A gentle rap at the front door startled him, and he turned to see Agent Rhodes. She had one hand cupped to the window and was peering in.

Lockhart took his time to go over to the door and click the deadbolt open. He pushed the door open, and Caitlyn greeted him with a gentle smile.

"Long time, no see," she said. "Joy said you might be here."

Lockhart stepped to the side to let her come in and returned to his place at the dinner counter.

Caitlyn sat next to him. "How are your ribs?"

Lockhart touched his side gently. "Still a bit tender. Ankle hurts worse. Haven't been able to run."

"Bummer. How's Scotty doing?" she asked innocently.

Lockhart raised his eyebrows and nodded slightly. "Good. He's a strong kid. They treated him for malnutrition and dehydration. He had a minor infection from where that psycho took off his hand, but he's doing good. It's only been three days, and they're already saying he can leave the hospital soon."

"What about his hand?"

Lockhart shrugged. "They talked about trying to reattach it, but something came up in the toxicology results for Vlad's blood that spooked them away from that plan. He's probably better without it. Who knows what that could do to a kid? The psycho cut off his hand and attached it to his own just to plant fingerprints. Not sure I would even want it back if it were me."

Caitlyn nodded. "Yeah, I guess it'll all be pretty hard to deal with, but now he only has one hand."

Lockhart looked down at his coffee. "It coulda been worse. Like I said, he's a tough kid."

The two sat in silence as Lockhart slowly sipped his coffee.

"I suppose you heard about the investigation into my actions," Lockhart said, finally breaking the silence.

"Yeah. That's actually kind of why I'm here." Caitlyn turned and looked at him. "I want you to know that my report stated only what actually happened, and it was my feeling that you deserved a commendation for your efforts—"

"I know," Lockhart said, cutting her off.

Caitlyn stopped and stared at the Crayton police chief. "You *know*?"

Lockhart took another long, slow sip. "Yeah. I spent the morning talking to my old boss, Assistant Director Chalmers, in DC."

Caitlyn sat waiting as Lockhart had evidently stopped speaking. "And?" she said with barely contained curiosity.

"Well," Lockhart said as he got up and walked around the counter to refill his coffee, "He said you spoke very highly of my capacity as an investigator. Thanks for that, by the way." Lockhart returned to his seat and slowly drizzled cream into his cup. "Then he said, given my long service record and 'outstanding dedication to both job and country,' not only will they not be pursuing legal actions, but they're also reconsidering my transfer. Pending a new psychological analysis to determine what they seem to find as 'a newfound capacity to handle the difficulties of homicide investigation,' my old job is waiting for me."

Agent Rhodes sat with her mouth agape at the news. "Uh...congratulations," she said, leaning forward, though not entirely sure if she should give him a hug or a pat on the back.

"What for?" Lockhart asked, not nearly as moved by the news as she was.

Caitlyn sat back in confusion. "What do you mean? For getting your job back, of course."

Lockhart shook his head. "I didn't take it."

Agent Rhodes blinked, and that was about all. She waited for an explanation or a follow-up, but none came. There was no punch line to his joke, and she found that unnerving and incredible. "What do you mean you didn't take it? Why not?" she asked in utter disbelief.

Lockhart set his coffee cup down and looked at the counter. He hadn't made eye contact with her since she'd come to the diner door. "See if you can follow me on this one, Agent Rhodes. I spent nearly twenty years of my life with the Bureau. I was a highly decorated special agent with an *impeccable* service record. Then I got assigned to a case in Crayton. I tracked down and killed a guy who raped and murdered kids. After that, the same Bureau I sacrificed my social life or any would-be family for made a decision based on some shrink's report that I was no longer fit for active duty."

Lockhart slowly spun his coffee cup as he

ruminated. "Then, for reasons I still can't figure out, I was assigned to take over as chief of police in a town I hadn't heard of till weeks prior."

There was another long slurp of coffee before he went on, "Another six weeks, and I found a missing kid and a guy who'd been mutilating people for who knows how long. Even Chalmers seemed to think they could link Vlad or whoever he was to a lot more than just went on here. They are looking into cold cases in Nashville as we speak. And now, all the sudden, I'm fit for duty again? What changed?"

The question hung in the air; it was one Rhodes had no answer for.

Lockhart finally looked up, his eyes clear, a smile almost on his face. His posture had made him look sad or depressed, but his face looked as tranquil as Rhodes had ever seen anyone look. "I changed. I really did. I didn't think the people here would grow on me, but between Jill, Joy, Freddie, and everyone else, life changed without me even realizing it. I mean, Scotty might be dead now and others too if...well, you know. No offense."

Rhodes shook her head. "None taken."

"I guess as much as I want to think of myself as an FBI agent, it's just not who I am anymore. After I saw Scotty on that table, the look in the kid's eyes..." Lockhart trailed off and stared at nothing for a moment. "When I saw that, I realized I can't leave here. In the last six weeks, two serial killers have been linked to the people of this town. God willing, that'll be all, but I can't leave them now. Maybe this is a place where I can finally settle down—a place where I can finally just be happy to be...just a cop."

Caitlyn swiveled in her chair and looked out the

diner door to the empty town streets just beyond. "I never thanked you, you know," Rhodes said as she stood and straightened her suit coat.

Lockhart looked into her eyes thoughtfully. "You're welcome."

"We got pretty lucky that we all didn't go down when the place blew."

Lockhart shrugged again. "Yeah, but Chalmers said the explosion wasn't meant for us or Vlad. The explosives were attached to machinery all over the factory. I guess it was pretty advanced stuff—stuff that even the Bureau techs were going to take a while to sort through. Some of it was decades ahead of what we're using now." Lockhart's fingers traced an invisible pattern on the Formica countertop. "I suppose we'll never really know what went on there. It was way above me," Lockhart said hollowly, words he'd been forced to say more than a few times in his professional life. "I talked with a doctor who said it takes weeks or months to heal from a hand transplant. This guy did it in a day. Doc said young men are perfect donors because of the elasticity of their skin, overall health, and testosterone levels. I-I just don't know what to think about it."

Caitlyn sat in the silence, letting the ominous cloud of the statement linger. "So maybe he wasn't as crazy as we thought."

Lockhart laughed for the first time around Rhodes and for the first time in he didn't know how long.

"What's so funny?" Caitlyn asked, almost offended.

"Nothing. Sorry. It's kind of an inside thing." Lockhart's mind drifted to his predecessor, John Donaldson. "Just seems like crazy goes hand in hand with the things that go on in this town." Lockhart cleared his throat and composed himself, then said, "The guy was crazy. Don't get that confused. I'm sure the world is better off with him dead on a slab."

Caitlyn looked over at Lockhart, not entirely sure if he was being cynical or a realist. Finally, she walked back over to the café door and hesitated at the handle.

"You know," Lockhart said without turning, "you did good work. You're a good agent. I would have never even been part of the case if it hadn't been for your instincts."

Caitlyn smiled. "Give me a call sometime, Chief," she said invitingly over her shoulder.

Lockhart turned to face her, his eyebrows raised.

She smiled coyly and added, "If you ever need a hand, I mean." And with that, Caitlyn left Lockhart alone and walked out the door, into the quiet streets of Crazytown.

Epilogue

A placid whistle echoed around the coroner's autopsy room. It had been a long day, but Dr. Joshua Driver was cruising through it pretty well. All the more exciting, he was about to do an autopsy on a John Doe who appeared to have suffered from some fairly serious dimorphic issues.

Initial inspection showed that both the left and right hand had been replaced. The left hand had been done fairly recently; however, the progression of healing was unlike anything Driver had ever seen.

Massive damage on and around the face were largely caused by the impact of the deceased through glass windows. Additional scar tissue was found around the face, and on closer inspection, it appeared that the tissue around the jaw line didn't match the tissue of the face itself.

There were additional discrepancies in the skin. From limb to limb, there appeared to be differences between the aging and elasticity of the skin. There was also a great deal of scar tissue at the joints of the legs and arms. His torso also showed multiple incision scars.

Not only that, but the body itself weighed nearly 400 pounds. Given the height at around six-one and the low body fat, it didn't seem possible, even with the impressive amount of muscle mass he carried. The age had first been estimated between twenty-five and thirty years old, but the variances in skin and weight made a pinpoint impossible. Only further inspection of the internal organs would reveal more consistent patterns of aging.

Dr. Driver couldn't remember another time when he'd been so excited to perform an autopsy, if for no other reasons than to see what else he might find.

The initial inspection had been interesting enough. There were copper protrusions all along the base of the neck and spine. They were more than cosmetic implants, as there seemed to be scoring from intense burns around each implant site, as if caused by strong electrical currents.

First Driver slid the rubber body block under the back of the body, causing the arms and neck to fall backward and push the chest upward; this made it easier to make the thoracic incisions. Finally, after all the whispering and conjecture amongst his peers, it was time for the internal examination.

The cause of death had already been attributed to a gunshot wound to the chest in conjunction with the massive blood loss from two additional bullet wounds and the facial damage; however, an internal examination would be needed for confirmation.

Inspecting the internal organs had always been one of his favorite parts of the job. Gross anatomy and autopsy was tough even for guys who would go on to be surgeons, but for Driver, it was a thrill—a constant moment of discovery.

Driver started with the large, Y-shaped incision starting at the top of each shoulder and running down the front of the chest. The incision was then extended all the way down to the pubic bone, making the usual deviation to the left side of the navel.

Driver set the surgical blade back on the tray, barely a drop of blood on the instrument. It was so much better than drowning victims, when bodies so often poured blood from all the pressure. He next grabbed the clean, polished shears to open the chest cavity.

Driver's intention was to saw through the ribs on the lateral sides of the chest cavity, until he was finally able to pull the sternum and attached ribs as one chest plate. Now, as often as ever, this part was crucial to allow a view of the heart and lungs and so that the heart in particular, given the established cause of death, and the pericardial sac would not be damaged or disturbed from opening.

That was his intention at least. However, as soon as he started to cut into the bone, he found that the shears weren't able to break through. Driver looked closer at the shears; they appeared to be in working order.

He set them aside and reached for the sternal saw, which was usually reserved for splitting the breastbone. With a couple of little revs, the blade was spun in a blur of cutting power. It was a personal favorite of his, capable of cutting through bone like particle board; however, even this tool seemed to have difficulty cutting through the ribs.

It actually took physical exertion for Driver to lean into the cuts and pop through each rib. The density of each bone was like nothing he'd seen before. There were several extra layers of calcification, which likely explained the unexpected weight of the body.

Driver grabbed the scalpel again to remove the still-attached soft tissue from the posterior side of the chest plate. Finally, the lungs and heart were exposed.

Wait...that can't be right. Driver did a double-take as he looked inside the chest cavity and spotted quite the abnormality there. It appeared as though there was a massive tumor just behind and to the side of the heart.

Driver looked deeper, and the scalpel in his hand

shuddered before falling to the ground. *It's just not...it isn't possible. There is no way it could be...*

Driver went immediately to the wall phone and dialed up his supervisor. "Dr. Weaver, this is Dr. Driver. I'm performing the autopsy on the John Doe from the FBI." Driver's voice dripped with urgency.

"Are you done already, Doctor?" Weaver asked nonchalantly.

"No, sir. I-I actually just started. The body's, uh...it's just that... Dr. Weaver, I think you oughtta get down here. There's something you need to see."

An audible sigh came through the receiver. "What is it, Driver?"

"Well, sir, I can't be certain until I look further and run tests, but it appears that the body has *two* hearts."

The response came quickly. "What? Did you say 'two hearts'? That's not possible, Doctor."

While the two men argued over the possibility of the John Doe having two hearts, it was clear that Dr. Driver hadn't taken a close enough inspection of the body before calling his supervisor. If he had, he would have noticed that not only did Vlad in fact have two hearts, but the second was faintly beating.

While Dr. Driver argued on the phone as to whether or not he'd be granted credit for the discovery and subsequent publishing possibilities, he failed to notice that he'd been doing an autopsy on a *living* body with a still-beating pulse. He also failed to notice when Vlad's hand reached out to the surgical table for a needle and sutures....

The End

ABOUT THE AUTHOR

Jon is a graduate of the University of Minnesota Duluth English Department as well as the Hamline University MFA: Writing program. He currently resides in Minnesota. His first book *Crazytown* is available on Amazon.com and BN.com.

Made in the USA
Lexington. KY
03 February 2014